# THE CRIPPLED TANKER

## by

## D. A. Rayner

**THUNDERCHILD PUBLISHING**
Huntsville, Alabama

**THE CRIPPLED TANKER**

Copyright © 1960 by D. A. Rayner.

Published by agreement with the Denys Rayner Trust.

ISBN-13: 978-1518809255
ISBN-10: 1518809251

Published by Thunderchild Publishing.  Find us at
https://ourworlds.net/thunderchild_cms/

# Table of Contents

# *Chapter 1*

*The action takes place in February 1943*

John Murrell, commanding His Majesty's Destroyer *Hecate,* had jammed himself into the port forward corner of the open bridge, and, in order to lessen his height and bring his head below the level of the glass windscreen, one leg was bent and the other stretched out to where his foot could obtain a purchase against the edge of the plinth that surrounded the standard compass. The wind, cold and rain-sodden, whipped the spray from the port bow wave and forced him to keep his head at a permanent tilt. In this way his shoulder supported him when the ship rolled to port, while his foot took the strain of the heavier roll to lee ward.

The *Hecate,* which had spent the night astern of the convoy, was moving up to her day station on the port bow of the merchantmen. Steaming at twenty knots, with the sea on her beam, she rolled heavily. The waves of her wash meeting the greater waves of the Atlantic raised pinnacles of water along the weather side, and even when they fell back into their own element without crashing against her, the wind seized their tops and flung the spray like shot across the low hull. Water, salt mixed with rain, ran all over her. Her own vibration and the flutterings of the wind formed it into glistening runnels that were repetitive in form. They lay like varnish that has been applied too thickly, and like varnish they glistened in the pale light of the new day.

In a similar posture and at a decent distance, Bill Wheeler, the First Lieutenant, crouched behind his captain. Sea-booted and oilskinned, his sou'wester pulled well down to shield his face, he had for the moment nothing to do. Murrell, as always, had come up to take the ship through the convoy, and, although both were well aware that the Executive Officer was quite capable of doing so alone, custom dictated that the Captain should be there — and so he was.

But it was not, Murrell reflected, entirely custom that brought him on deck at first light each day. As the war dragged on and he became more and more senior and graduated to larger and more important commands, the opportunities of actually handling his own ship became fewer and fewer. In his trawler, with only two other officers — and neither trained — he had had to oversee everything. In his corvette there had been one other trained officer and the other two had been learners, but the *Hecate* had no less than fourteen officers in the wardroom. There were even two officers for each watch, the senior of whom was always experienced. Except for this morning run through the convoy, actual physical control of his ship fell to him only on the infrequent occasions when they were in contact with the enemy, or when they were entering or leaving harbour — and in the first case he was far too busy to squeeze enjoyment from ship handling.

"How much further to go, Sub?" Keeping his head still, the Captain spoke sideways to the Second Officer of the Watch. He was not prepared to give the spray a chance to climb down his neck. Sub-Lieutenant Sampson stirred from the trancelike state to which cold and the anticipation of breakfast had reduced him, and began to shuffle around the standard compass to take a bearing of the leading merchant ship of the port column. As he bent to look along the pylorus, Murrell wondered whether or not the lad — he was just twenty — would have the sense to ask the Radar Office for a range, and then report both range and bearing so that his captain would know the exact position. Sampson leaned over and raised the lid of the voice pipe that led to the Radar Office. Murrell thought that now everyone was so well trained his own job was losing interest.

"Bearing two-eight-two degrees: range two thousand," Sampson said.

Murrell, shifting position, said to Wheeler, "Near enough. You carry on. Normal convoy speed. Normal zigzag."

Wheeler, too, released himself from the posture of rest. He stepped onto the plinth by the compass and called down the voice pipe to the wheelhouse. "One-one-oh revolutions. Steer oh-three-oh."

6

Murrell, feeling the ship begin to lose speed and move less violently, stood upright and looked round. "I was going to say 'just the same as always,' " he remarked conversationally to Wheeler, "but of course we're missing the big tanker this morning. What was her name?"

*"Antioch,"* Wheeler told him, "a Greek." Despite the foul conditions, the morning's run through the convoy had given Murrell a pleasurable sensation. It was intensely interesting to pass through the ranks of the convoy. Then ships which from a mile or two outside the formation had appeared as nothing more than a crowd would be seen to have their own individuality. It was as if a bird had swooped down to have a closer look at the shoppers in a street and been given a glimpse of what was in the shopping baskets.

There were many ships with deck cargoes: tanks, motor transport and small specialized landing-craft. It was heartening to exchange a friendly wave with the officers of the ships they passed. It brought a touch of human warmth to the whole bloody business of war.

"What went wrong last night, sir?" Wheeler asked.

"He must have come in from just about where we are now," Murrell told him, referring to the U-boat that had done the damage. "Right between the two corvettes. Perhaps someone's radar wasn't working, or some operator not watching the set. But conditions were pretty bad — it may have been just luck that let him through. This ship has nothing to blame itself for. It's just a disappointment for us all — and I bet our Senior Officer is mad about it. The biggest ship in the convoy, and bang in the middle! Just look how her going alters the whole seascape. She was like the hub of a wheel. We were so used to her being there."

*"Bruce* has been signalling to the rescue ship for the last half hour," Wheeler said. "I could read a bit of the signal before we'd got too far up the convoy to see the light. It seems they got the crew off her."

Although the Senior Officer's lamp had not been trained on them, they had for some minutes been able to see its continual flickering. Now *Bruce* was receiving a long message from the rescue ship that was stationed astern of the convoy. But there were ships in

7

the way, and the officers on the *Hecate's* bridge could not read the words.

Then suddenly, and all at once, *Bruce's* lamp was trained on them. "Yeoman!" the Captain called. But it was a needless warning. Willis, the Senior Signal Rating, was always on deck for the morning reshuffle of stations. He was already at the lamp.

Murrell, as relieved as the ship from the tension of high speed, moved slowly into the chart house, which, like an enlarged dog kennel, formed a low shelter across the front of the bridge and jutted out over the wheelhouse below. There he took from his pocket the tin in which he kept his cigarettes and gratefully inhaled the smoke. Then, intending to discuss the repainting of the mess decks, he called his first lieutenant: "Number One!"

But it was the Yeoman who first appeared, pad in hand, in the low doorway. A flurry of wind fluttered the pages as he held the signal for Murrell to read. The Captain took the pad and laid it on the chart table before him. "Senior Officer 40th Escort Group to *Hecate*," Murrell read. "I have formed the opinion that Greek tanker *Antioch* is still afloat and could probably be towed to U.K. Survivors' reports indicate that ship was floating well when abandoned. Only engine room seems to have been hit. Fire confined to fuel-oil tanks port side. Cargo tanks undamaged. You are to return and if practicable you are to take her in tow until relieved by ocean tug."

The Captain looked up from the pad. The First Lieutenant's interested face peered over the Yeoman's shoulder. "Damn and blast! What does he think we are — a bloody tugboat?" Murrell exploded. "Surely he could have given a towing job to a corvette. They are at least fitted for it!"

"It'll be a change, sir." Wheeler attempted to offer sympathy.

"Oh, yes," Murrell snapped, "you'll have lots of fun handling wires and hawsers. Interesting — very interesting on a summer's day in peacetime when that sort of manoeuvre is practiced. It will be a nightmare job in a North Atlantic winter. And anyway, I don't like the idea of being tied by the backside to a floating oil well. Not when the enemy may still be hanging around. It's too good a target altogether."

8

"You really think she'll be fit to tow?" Wheeler asked.

"I'm afraid so. When we first saw the flames last night they looked bad enough — one can't blame the Greeks for getting out quick. But when you compare them with some of the other bangs we've seen, you'll realize that the main cargo tanks just can't have been punctured. Remember the blowing up of the *Tapico!*"

And Wheeler, standing beside his captain, saw in memory's brightest mirror the vision of flame in the dark which would so often surprise him at unexpected moments with a vividness he knew no years of life would dim or salve. A picture always matched by another: the picture of that same ship in dry dock. Then her vast bulk had made her seem indestructible — as if no force on earth could have disintegrated her within the mere second it had taken.

A signalman put his head through the doorway. "Signal from *Bruce,* sir," he said, and added, "Private prefix."

Then Murrell knew that it was a personal message from one captain to another.

"I bet you're sucking your teeth," the new signal read, "but if the job is hopeless you can get back much more quickly than a corvette. It may be quite a big decision to make so I'm afraid it's your honour to go. Good luck."

"Well," Murrell said, handing the signal to Wheeler, "that sweetens the pill a little, but not much. Bring her round to two-seven-oh, Number One. Speed twenty knots, and get the Navigator to give you an exact course for the wreck."


As soon as he had seen the *Hecate* settled on a course that would take her back to the position where the tanker had been torpedoed, Murrell left the bridge to go down to his sea-cabin on the deck below.

Halfway down the ladder he paused to look at the ships in convoy. The strong west wind whipped the smoke from their funnels and, heavy with rain, pressed it close to the surface ahead of the rolling merchantmen. Watching them drop astern of his own racing destroyer, he felt a strong disinclination to quit their company. Here there were friends who in an emergency could be relied upon to

9

come to his aid. Beyond the horizon, where winter waves snatched at the sky, there would only be an empty ship in an ocean that harboured enemies. Alone, his ship was capable of looking after herself. There were many previous occasions when he'd been detached on some errand or other, and these departures had heralded possible adventure. But to be chained by the leg to a tow was something quite different. It came to him that he was hoping the confounded tanker had already sunk and, though he tried hard to suppress this, he knew it was true.

A more than usually heavy plunge of the ship's bow sent an extra-heavy sheet of spray across the bridge. A spatter found its way down the companionway. Murrell, wiping his face, jumped the last two rungs of the ladder and hurried into his sea-cabin.

Kirby, his steward, was already there. The fiddles that held the dishes had been fixed to the folding flap that served as a table, and under the cover that had been set in the central square would be a plate of bacon and eggs. He wondered whether, on this particular morning, he was as interested in breakfast as usual. The ship flung her bow upward and Kirby swayed forward. Murrell clutched the doorpost to prevent himself being catapulted back into the passage. The two men smiled at each other, not as captain and man, but as two human beings confined by fate in the same small reeling box and forced to bow to one another.

"Chucking herself around this morning," Kirby said.

"I'm in a hurry," Murrell told him as he took off his damp duffel-coat and flung it on the bunk, and his wet cap after it.

Kirby, as he retrieved the wet clothing and hung it up on the hook behind the door, made a clicking sound with tongue against teeth. "Hear we got a towing job, sir."

Murrell, ignoring the rebuke Kirby had managed to imply, was grateful for the tidying of his cabin. He sat down heavily in the chair before the table. So it was around the ship already; hardly surprising, he supposed. Any departure from the normal must be the cause of anxious comment. A job! A job? What sort of a job? Where are we going now? Someone would tell someone else, and then everybody would know. "If it's still afloat," Murrell said, trying to be noncommittal. He had no wish that his private thoughts on the subject should be relayed around the ship as quickly as the other information had been.

Kirby, a coffee pot in one hand and the doorpost in the other, held the pot waveringly towards the Captain's cup. "No, thank you," Murrell said. "Don't pour it out yet." Kirby had been a stableboy before the war and now fussed over Murrell as he had once looked after his horses. It was an attitude that the Captain sometimes found exasperating, and as often appreciated. This morning was one of the in-between times. He said, "She's throwing herself about too much. Stand the jug in the wastepaper basket. It'll stay quiet there."

Murrell had heard the clattering feet on the iron ladder that told of the change of the watch: the feet that climbed steadily up and the feet that, after four hours on deck, ran hurriedly down to the warmth of the mess decks. Wheeler would already be sitting at the head of the wardroom table at the other end of the ship. As Kirby went out of the door, Murrell called, "Kirby. My compliments to the First Lieutenant, and will he come and see me here as soon as he's had his breakfast." He supposed he had about half an hour to get his own mind clear on the issue, and began to hurry the food into his mouth.

He had hardly finished, and was considering whether to try to drink his coffee at the table or to sit on the edge of the bunk where he could swing his body in time with the ship, when there was a knock on the door. "Come in," he called and then, "Oh, it's you, Doc. And what does the medical adviser want at this hour of the morning?"

"I could do with a case," Macmillan said. "A nice difficult diagnosis — something to make my brain work."

"I know," Murrell said, well aware of his friend's complaint. "Your father and mother stinted themselves for your education, and now a broken finger or a simple case of skin disease is all you're ever asked to mend. See! I've said it for you. Come in and help me think."

"What about?" Macmillan said as he perched himself on the bunk.

"It's no use pretending you don't listen to rumour and it's no use saying you don't know."

"You mean this towing job?" Macmillan grinned. "Maybe she's sunk."

"Frankly, and just between you and me, I hope she has. I don't fancy it."

"Why not?"

Murrell paused while he poured himself a cup of coffee and joined the doctor on the bunk. "I don't think I'm psychologically fitted to be a tug-master in wartime! It calls for a special sort of courage that I don't think I've got. And even if I had, it would be devoured by my phobia about being tied up."

"Is it different from any other kind of courage?" Macmillan asked.

"I'd say it's quite different from any we normally call upon in war. It's got to go on for so long! Continual fear draws courage from men as surely as sun evaporates water. For most of us there's a period fixed by the duration and extent of the ordeal — different for each one. I've only had to tow once — that was with my trawler — a damaged destroyer halfway home from Dunkirk. Then the sea was full of all sorts of craft going the same way, and the German airmen were as tired as we were. This won't be the same at all. There are lots of people, Doc, who, if they had to, could die a damn fine gladiator's death, but who'd put up a pretty poor show as a martyr. How the devil do you take a big merchantman in tow with a destroyer?"

"Aren't there diagrams and directions in the books?"

"Oh yes, lots of them. But they all refer to towing battleships and suppose that the tow has steam on her capstan. And however much a naval ship is disabled, she'll have a large number of beefy sailors to haul the heavy stuff around. With this *Antioch* we'll have to do the whole thing ourselves — and put men aboard her."

"How many will you have to send?" the doctor wanted to know.

"Unless the weather improves a great deal — and the glass is still dropping a tenth an hour — no more than can be ferried in one boatload. But that brings me to the most difficult decision of the lot. Who to send in charge of them?"

"Who will you?"

"I don't know," Murrell said, "and the hell of it is that I must make up my mind before Wheeler comes up. It would hardly be fair to make him a party to that discussion."

"Why not Thompson?" the doctor asked.

"He's too unreliable, too pleased with himself. You could never really trust any report he made. All the information that comes to us from the *Antioch* will be sent through the one officer's brain. I daren't have someone there who's like a pendulum — swinging too far each way."

"But," Macmillan said, "your choice really lies between Bill Wheeler and Thompson. So you've answered your own question!"

Murrell nodded. "By rights I shouldn't send my Executive Officer out of the ship — but I'll have to. And that's another thing I'm going to hate. We've been together some years now. He was one of the two sub-lieutenants that commissioned the *Orchid* with me in December, 1940. I was lucky to get him as first lieutenant for this ship. It's wonderful what you can do when the 'appointments' people get to know you! But it makes the worry more personal if you have to send someone you know so well and like so much to sit on top of four million gallons of high-octane petrol when you can't really give him proper defence against either aircraft or U-boats."

"Is there really as much petrol as that?" Macmillan asked.

Murrell, still thinking of the explosion that might project his friend into eternity, said, "What are a few thousand gallons more or less? They'd make little difference to the size of the bang. Work it out for yourself. A fourteen-thousand-ton tanker carries about that weight of oil. That's nearly four million gallons — enough to send two thousand Wellington bombers to Berlin and back. Makes you think, doesn't it? You begin to realize just how important escort work can be."

"Even towing work, for that matter." The doctor seized the opportunity to support his captain's determination.

"Or towing." Murrell had to admit the rise of interest. But then, with the return of apprehension, "Burning's not so funny! You hadn't joined us when the *Tapico* was hit, had you? That shook me. It shook us all...." He spoke quietly, more to himself than to an audience.

13

Macmillan had heard the tale from others, never from the Captain. The doctor, seeing this retelling as an effort by the other man to remove a horror from his mind, knew it would be only a temporary palliative. There were some thoughts no confidant could relieve.

"... It was on a black and friendly night. The sort of night when the soft drizzle makes it seem almost cosy on the bridge, as if your ship had been wrapped up and decently hidden from the enemy. One of the wing corvettes had reported a radar contact some minutes before. But he hadn't seemed certain of it, and, as there were a lot of false echoes about, no one had really believed that there was a U-boat there. Of course, the Senior Officer had had to do something. I'd been told to go and help the corvette. We were on the way, going through the convoy — my thoughts much more on dodging the darkened ships than on the Germans, and hoping like hell that no trigger-happy sailor in a merchantman would mistake me for a submarine and shoot me up — when the ship alongside me was hit...."

Murrell paused and, as if his glance had shifted from one object to another, moved his head. But Macmillan knew that his companion had gone back eight months in time and neither saw nor felt anything of the present.

"... A big tanker — big as the *Antioch* — and almost new. Oddly enough, Wheeler and I had seen her in dry dock when we were refitting on the *Clyde* some months before. Then, on a quiet Sunday afternoon, we'd walked all around and underneath her like ants under a wheelbarrow, and wondered at the enormous bulk of her. You wouldn't think, you know, that something men had built as big as that could disappear. Even to have thought of her doing so would have seemed sacrilegious — as if, in doubting her indestructibility, one doubted God, who'd let man build her.

"And yet, in something less than a second, she went. There was a flicker of flame in the dark, and then beside us a wall of fire hundreds of feet high all wound about and patterned with black smoke. In the fraction of time between one and the other, like a silent motion picture played slowly, we saw her tanks burst one after the other, until all her length was one great silent blaze. To this day,

I don't know where the noise went. It was so quiet. And then, in the awful hush, we heard her men crying — a drawn-out wail you'd not think could come from human throats. I don't ever want to hear *that* again."

The doctor took out his pipe and rubbed the bowl against the side of his nose, then paused to look at the polish this had given the wood. It was a mannerism to which he frequently resorted when in thought, and one that often left a smudge on the side of his nose. "You know, it might be as well to put that on the ship's notice board," Macmillan, trying to sound matter-of-fact, said. "I mean about the amount of petrol in the *Antioch* and how many bombers it would take to Berlin. I bet not a single man in the ship has realized the size of this endeavour."

"It's an idea," Murrell agreed. "Until you made me figure it out, I don't think I'd realized it myself."

The doctor slid himself off the bunk. "I'll be getting along. There's a very interesting case in the sick bay for my morning's work. A split fingernail — a little finger, mark you. Not even a thumb!"

"Never mind," Murrell told him, "you make a damn fine mess secretary — and you're a great moral support for me."

## Chapter 2

When the doctor had left, Murrell went into the chart room, a cabin that matched his own on the other side of the bridge. The dark polished-wood desk with its big drawers, the rexine-covered settee in its wood frame, the glint of reflected light from the bright metal of star globe, sextant and chronometer, in contrast to the white paintwork of his own cabin, gave the place a Victorian atmosphere. Masters, the Navigator, was bent over the table. He stood up and faced the Captain. "Barometer?" Murrell asked.

"Twenty-nine and two tenths: falling about a tenth each hour, sir."

"No star-sight this morning, Pilot." Murrell's words were a complaint about the weather, not a question.

"No, sir. And not much chance of seeing the sun today. But I had quite good stars last night."

"Did you?" Murrell said. "That would be only about two hours before the *Antioch* was 'fished.' So our guess at her position should be pretty good, and give us a chance to find her in time."

Murrell, looking at the gentle and scholarly Navigator, thought how outward appearance could often indicate the work a man would do best. A spasm of jealousy flicked through the Captain's mind. In his trawler, and again in the corvette, he'd been both captain and navigator. In the destroyer he had a specialist officer to do the job for him, and somehow that seemed a pity. Although he was admittedly responsible for the whole working of the ship, the thrills of navigational success now came to him second-hand. He wished that, beside berthing the ship in harbour, there was something to do that was all his own, that depended entirely on his own ability. "What's the approximate distance of the *Antioch* from Bloody Foreland?" he asked.

"Five hundred miles, sir."

"Have we had the weather forecast?"

"Not yet, sir. The wireless office should be sending it up soon. I'll decode and plot it right away."

"Good," Murrell said. "Bring it to me in my cabin as soon as it's done."

Returning to his own cabin, he met Wheeler. "Come in, Number One, and let's prepare our thoughts for taking the Greek in tow. We've got to assume she's afloat and be as ready as possible. If we aren't, we'll not get the tow secured before dark, and that would be a pity. We certainly don't want to show lights at night." Murrell turned away. It was, he found, extremely difficult to avoid the implication of danger. How was he to tell Wheeler that, if the *Antioch* was still afloat, it was most likely the torpedo that had done the damage was a magnetic one that had exploded beneath the ship's bottom; but with the *Hecate* tied up like a dog in a farmyard, the next attack would be made with torpedoes arranged to explode on contact?

He felt like a judge asked to pass sentence on a friend. But a judge would never have to do that. He'd have the case transferred to another court. There was no such escape for him. His association with Wheeler was compounded of usage and respect for a man who, his junior by ten years, shared his love for their ship. Knowledge of how a man would react to every conceivable situation brought trust; and at sea that was all-important. Murrell thought that he had learned more of Wheeler than he'd have learned in a lifetime ashore. It was a relationship that was quite different from his friendship with the doctor, who was nearer to him in age than any other of his officers. Macmillan was, so it seemed, part of the crew but additional to the ship, and so could be used as a confidant in a way that no one concerned with ship's duties could be. Knowing the doctor less intimately than he knew Wheeler made confidences easier to give and receive.

"I must have someone I can trust in the tow. I think you'd better take charge of the party." Murrell had to make a great effort to be natural.

"How long have I got to get ready?" Wheeler was matching his captain's detachment.

"The ship was torpedoed at eight o'clock last night. We turned back twelve hours later. She'd be about a hundred miles astern of the convoy when we left them. If we can maintain this speed, we should have her in sight by one o'clock this afternoon. Then we'll have five hours of daylight in which to work."

Murrell settled himself in the chair. "Sit on the bunk," he told Wheeler, and, "Who'd you like to take with you? I'll leave the choice to you. I'd prefer not to send the boat across more than once. When it has put your party aboard, it can drop downwind and I'll pick it up. Two men and a coxswain should be enough to paddle the boat back. You can take three men and yourself in the stern sheets and three men for the other oars — that will give you a crew of six. It doesn't sound many for a fourteen-thousand-ton vessel — but so long as you've enough you don't want more. You'll need a signalman, a torpedo rating in case you can do anything with the electrics, a leading stoker or engine-room artificer — better ask the Chief whom he recommends — one leading seaman and two able seamen."

There was a tap at the door. Murrell called, "Come in, Masters." It was not only the time of the interruption but the gentleness of the knock that had suggested the caller's identity.

Masters, entering the small cabin, found the air already blue with tobacco smoke. The Captain, pipe in mouth, was wedged in the armchair before the knee-hole desk, with his knees against the desk edge. His body was half turned towards the First Lieutenant, who was sitting on his legs to jam himself into the head of the bunk. Both men looked up at the newcomer. Their eyes, more inquisitive than their tongues, asked the same question.

"Not so good, sir," Masters said. "There's a deep depression running along under the edge of the Arctic high. It's travelling east at twenty knots." He put the open weather chart on the Captain's desk, and, as the ship suddenly flung herself skywards, he bowed deeply.

"Hold on, Pilot," Murrell laughed and rose from his chair to peer out through the salt-caked glass of the scuttle in the after bulkhead. From there he could just see down the starboard side of the long main deck, and as he rubbed away the beaded moisture on

18

the inside of the glass the *Hecate's* bow rose again as she shot over the top of an Atlantic greyback. The wavetop, broken by her passage, became a mass of frothy lace — a sort of antimacassar that, torn and twisted by the wind, was laid over the mound of the wave. Then, as the ship's propellers bit deeply into the sea, it drifted quickly astern.

"Looks perfectly bloody." The Captain, reseating himself, pulled the weather chart before him. "Tell me, Pilot, how long is this pocket gale going to last?"

"Not long, sir. As you see, it's really only a secondary to the one we've just had."

"Then the sooner we can get to the northward and into that 'Arctic high' the better. The convoy is probably in it already. But there may be snow on the border between the two." Murrell, who had been talking mainly to Wheeler, turned back to Masters. "Thank you, Pilot," he said in dismissal.

When the door had shut, Murrell turned again to his first lieutenant. "Well, there you are, Number One. We've decided what to do — or try to do. The weather is going to do its best to muck up our plans by blowing somewhere between force six and seven during the night, but we should manage. I only wish I had some experience in towing."

"Looks as if, until the ocean tug arrives, we're both going to learn a lot."

Wheeler had spoken so casually that Murrell wondered whether the younger man's imagination had been dulled by his sense of adventure. He said, "Yes, as you say — until the tug arrives."

"You don't sound very hopeful, sir!" Wheeler's tone made the statement almost a question.

"There are so few tugs, and they've so much to do! As rare as taxis in London on a wet day. But when it's fine, you can't step off the pavement in the blackout without being run down by one with its flag up!" All at once the desire came to Murrell to turn time ahead by a week. Not that he particularly wanted to know what he would be doing. He just wanted assurance that they'd all be there to do it. And, once started, the digression seemed to have no end. His thoughts, like children escaping from school, ran home to his family.

19

There, conditioned by the back cloth, of his present concern, they dwelt on the omission rather than the pleasures. If only, on his last leave, he had worked a little harder, he'd have finished the wading pool under the big tree at the bottom of the lawn. What had then been put off quite casually now assumed a major importance — as important to him this moment as it would be next summer to Ginna and Peter. At eight and six years old, wading pools were very important things. He wished he'd completed the pool, and he wished his parting with Susan had been more satisfactory. It was always difficult to explain to a wife that the whole leave period could not be spent in her company: there was so much to be done for the ship that only he, the Captain, could get done. He repeated that with almost desperate determination, but could not avoid wondering whether the division of loyalty between ship and wife had been quite fair. Next time — if there was a next time ...

Wheeler's voice cut into his thoughts. "I'd like to get the towing hawser laid out before I send the hands to dinner, but while she's travelling at this speed it's not possible."

"Don't bother about that," Murrell told him. "We can get it out while you're paddling across to your first command. Go and get your party together."


Murrell had not finished the first course of his lunch when the bell above the head of his bunk buzzed angrily. Tipping back the chair onto two legs, he could just lift the handset from its hook. He spoke conversationally into the mouthpiece. "Captain's cabin."

At first he heard only the attenuated whine of the wind, and then Masters' voice against the continuous background of sound. "The Radar Office has reported a definite echo bearing red two-oh, ten thousand yards. The plot suggests that it's stationary. Shall I alter course?"

"Yes, please, Pilot. I'll be up." Murrell, replacing the handset, allowed his chair to fall back on its four legs. It had been too much to hope that the *Antioch* would have solved his problems by slipping down to the bed of the ocean.

Getting out of his chair reminded him of the one occasion on which he'd found himself in the corner of a boxing ring. It was an unpleasant thought, because very shortly afterwards he'd been carried ignominiously through the ropes. Shrugging his arms into the sleeves of his duffel-coat, he held on to the doorway while the *Hecate's* bow rose, and then, in the moment of pause before it fell, he made the short journey down the transverse passage to where the ladder led to the open deck above. The blackout curtain flapped angrily as an eddy of wind caught it, and then hung still. Before mounting the ladder, he turned aside into the chart room. The barometer swung there in its gimbals. It had fallen another tenth. He went back to the passage and climbed the ladder to the bridge.

The wind that met him was warmer than it had been when, a prey to impatience, he had last been up an hour before. With the big area of cold Arctic anticyclone so close to them, the unseasonal warmth was not a good sign. Everything in sight was gray: the painted furniture of the bridge, the lighter camouflage of the forward gun, the darker tone of the foredeck. Gray seas sweeping out of the gray drizzle, and even the wavetops, when they broke into foam, were seen through the rain not as white but as a lighter shade of gray. He climbed heavily up to the standard compass. "Can you see her yet?"

Masters raised his arm to point ahead of the ship, and then the Captain saw her clearly through the curtain of rain — and much nearer than he had expected. The nearness of the sighting to which they had been guided by radar was a measure of the limited visibility. The *Antioch* lay beam-on to their approach. Come upon suddenly and seen indistinctly, gray painted upon a gray sea, she appeared vast and, in her desolation, phantasmal. "You'd expect to see the waves pass clean through her," Murrell said, and Masters, standing beside his captain, found nothing odd in the remark.

"She's a bit down by the stern, sir." The Navigator was the first to speak.

"With a laden tanker it's difficult to tell. They've so little freeboard," Murrell answered, keeping his binoculars on the object of their quest. "She's not much damaged, and she's spewing out enough oil to stop the seas breaking. There's no seaman's reason why we shouldn't try to tow the brute. Ease her down to ten knots while I take a look around, and pass the word for the First Lieutenant."

Murrell lowered his binoculars and moved to the side of the bridge. As the *Hecate's* speed was reduced and she ceased to fling herself from crest to trough, the waves appeared smaller and more kind. Spray no longer swept in sheets over the dripping fo'c'sle, nor blew like smoke across the decks. Murrell, thinking that the moment for irrevocable decision was approaching, found that it had already passed — realized that it had never been a free decision. He had been ordered to do something and, as long as it was there to be done, he could not escape his fate. Only two circumstances might delay, but not cancel, the attempt to carry out the order: the sea might be too rough to put men aboard the *Antioch,* or a U-boat might join him in his inspection of the derelict. He would have been free to hunt a U-boat, and then perhaps, by the time that he had finished, the Admiralty would have sent a tug. But there was no U-boat to hunt.

They were passing close by the *Antioch.* From the height of the bridge he could look down on her wallowing hull. It was certain that, bad though the weather might he, the whaler could put men aboard her. Perception of things seen must pass through a human mind and be personalized by the medium through which they are filtered. He wondered what others were thinking.


"I don't know when I've seen anything worth a million and a half look nastier," Leading Seaman Thomas said to the group of men clustered in the shelter of the fo'c'sle by the door that led to the mess decks. From this lower level, that was a bare eight feet above the waterline, the deserted hulk of the *Antioch* appeared even more unwieldy than from their captain's viewpoint on the bridge twenty-five feet above them.

"An' who says she's worth that lot?" a voice asked, and another answered him, "Skipper says so. He's put a notice on the board. Million and a half, he says, and enough juice in her to fly two thousand bombers to Berlin."

"If she was mine, I'd sell her for a pint of bitter," Thomas said.

"You'd not even get that much from me, chum," Wilson, a seaman, told him. "As far as I'm concerned you could have the whole bloody lot for now't. No, I want to see my wife and kids again!"

"What's come over you?" Thomas asked. "You weren't worried about 'em yesterday."

"Maybe not," Wilson said. "Yesterday was an ordinary day. This here's a different kettle of fish altogether. Why, damn it, man, we'll be no better than a piece of cheese in a mousetrap!"

"So what?" Thomas said, and added, "so long as there ain't no flipping mice."

"Trust the Greeks to get out quick," Wilson said.

"And that's not fair," Thomas told him. "You saw her on fire last night — an' look at the mess it's made of her paint-work aft. You'd not have stopped to ask if it were only the fuel tanks that were afire — not with all that aviation stuff aboard. You'd have been out of her before *your* fat started to fry, and well you know it!"

"And what chance do you suppose there is of not being spotted out here?" Wilson, defeated in the matter of the Greeks, returned to his original complaint. "Don't the Jerries have aircraft on patrol? Blimey, they've only got to catch sight of us once, and they'll have us for a certain, one way or the other — aircraft or U-boats. If it's aircraft, they'll go for the tanker first; if it's a U-boat, it'll pick us off to start with and 'fish' the tanker when it feels like it. To tie ourselves up to that is nothing but sheer bloody suicide!"

"Oh, for Christ's sake!" a new voice said. "If you can't be cheerful, stow it. There's nothing any of us can do about it — not even the Skipper. He's got to do what he's told, same as you and me."

Wheeler climbed the ladder to the bridge. With an oilskin over his duffel-coat, a length of line around his middle, and pockets stuffed with hastily snatched articles, he looked like a badly made up parcel. "Your party ready?" Murrell asked.

23

"They're mustering by the whaler now, sir."

"Very good. I'll come down and have a word with them."
Murrell turned toward the compass platform and called, "Masters,
keep the ship circling the wreck until I'm back."

The First Lieutenant had already begun the descent of the
long ladder that led from the after end of the bridge direct to the
main deck. For a moment the Captain paused before he followed. He
had given no order to begin the preparations for the tow. The
inevitability of their having to attempt the enterprise must have been
as plain to Wheeler as it had been inescapable to him. He felt as if
the whole life of the ship, as yet hesitant but always expectant, was
beginning to flow through his veins, strengthening his decision. The
ship was as deeply committed as if the whole Board of Admiralty
had considered and ordered the venture — but, over and above that
and far beyond it in urgency, his ship was committing herself. He
went quickly down the ladder to where Wheeler awaited him.

Together they walked slowly to the whaler. "Don't forget,
Number One," Murrell said, "that the merchantman is drifting
through the water at almost two knots. There'll be a big undertow on
her lee side. Don't get your boat broadside on to the ship. There are
some falls hanging from a davit on her lee quarter. If you can get in
under those you may be able to climb up a ladder that's over the side
there. Don't risk smashing your rudder. For that reason alone, it's
probably best to keep your bows up to the wreck." Murrell, sure that
Wheeler was fully aware of the necessity for all he'd said, wondered
why it had had to be said at all. Communication was not always
limited to just what the words said. Speech could be a hand
expressing friendship or encouragement. They came to a stop by the
whaler.

Fallen in abreast of the boat were nine of the best, and
certainly the strongest, men in the ship. The Captain ran his eye over
them quickly, assessing each in turn. Hart, the engine-room artificer,
a dependable honest man with a wife and two children. Signalman
White, a big laughing youngster who would be very difficult to
dishearten. Leading Seaman Pengelley, the best seaman in the ship,
not perhaps quite up to the weight of the others, but as tough as a
man could be. Murrell thought that Wheeler had been right so far.

He was not so certain of the next: Sibson, torpedoman, was a nuisance in the ship. He was big enough and strong enough to match the rest of the party, but his punishment record was bad and he had trouble at home.

And there were two able seamen: Trotman, a hulk of a man who would be as brave as a lion because he hadn't the imagination to be otherwise; and Anders, a flaxen-haired giant who, though he sometimes appeared simple-minded, had, in affairs of the sea, a quite uncanny knack of doing the right thing by instinct. With Pengelley and Anders in his crew, Murrell thought that Wheeler had taken the best he could lay his hands on — and those who would have been the most use on the *Hecate*. But the dispatch of any picked crew must lower the efficiency of those that remained.

Each of these six men carried a parcel done up in waterproof cloth. This and their heavier clothing distinguished them from the three men who would make the return journey to the destroyer. "Richards," Murrell said, "you're coxswain of the boat. When you've put the party aboard, row downwind. When you see me closing you, turn your boat around and keep her heading about twenty degrees off the wind. I'll pick you up — don't you start chasing me. If I miss you the first time, I'll try again." And then to the six, "You men of the towing party: don't forget that from the moment you leave this ship Mr. Wheeler is your commanding officer — and don't worry. I'm sure that between us we'll manage the tow."

Murrell turned to Wheeler and offered his hand. "Good luck, Number One," he said, forcing himself to look into his first lieutenant's face. Then a thought came to save banalities. "My apologies. Good luck — Captain."

## Chapter 3

"I'd dearly love to be taking a trip in the boat," Macmillan said to Murrell as the Captain took the ship upwind of the wreck to slip the whaler. The doctor, who had watched the preparations at the boat, had followed the Captain up to the bridge, where he was always a welcome and self-effacing visitor. Like a spider's web his perception ran through the ship, and he was ideally suited to be the dispassionate observer. It was a position he enjoyed, and, if he grumbled at the lack of medical work, he had no complaint of the interest his naval rank had brought to his bachelor life.

Towing and salvage had always seemed to him the highest exposition of a seaman's art. But perhaps, because he had only been a ship's doctor for a comparatively quiet two months, he had not been long enough at sea for the constant awareness of the enemy to have eaten into his mind — an awareness in which each thought, conscious or subconscious, became conditioned by the threat of their presence. It had been with some surprise that he sensed the revulsion of feeling throughout the ship whenever the tow was mentioned. "You know," he went on, speaking to the Captain, "what I've always most wanted to do was to sail my wee yacht across the Atlantic. Perhaps when the war is over, and before I go back to the hospital, I'll do just that."

"Alone?" Murrell asked, as he kept his eyes on the sea, the *Antioch* and the behaviour of his own ship.

"Yes," the doctor said. "I'd prefer it that way. Just think of the utter isolation, the blessed solitude. Out there and alone you could really think things out!" He waved a hand over a gray and empty arc of the sea.

"You couldn't," Murrell said. "I've tried it. Not on such a long trip as that. Only from Scotland to Norway and back — and shortish hops round the coast. But it doesn't work out. Your mind is full of the minute-by-minute problems the yacht creates: the set of the sails, the necessity to make little repairs, and the job of getting the next meal while at the same time you look after the ship. I'm afraid the best forcing ground for philosophy is a nice dry hut on the beach, with food and wine brought at regular intervals by a docile slave. Any day I'd back Diogenes' land-based tub against your seagoing one!"

"You disappoint me," Macmillan said. "Without a wife I could take time off and accept the risk."

Murrell said to the wheelhouse, "Steer five degrees to starboard," and to the doctor, "I reckon we'll be ready to slip the boat very soon. Why are you a bachelor?" And he thought how one could, when men were busy, sometimes ask personal questions that would be very difficult to broach even when alone with a friend and a bottle of wine.

"A defect in my own character." Macmillan spoke frankly. "I can't accept interference in my own work — either active or passive. That's why I like singlehanded sailing, why I prefer working in a hospital to being in practice."

"But, good God, hospitals are full of women!"

Macmillan laughed. "But the nursing staff do what they are told, at the same time as they control the worse vagaries of the female patients."

Murrell said, "I'm going to slip the boat now. But I don't see how you're going to be much of a philosopher unless you accept the coexistence of women. Slow ahead. Steady as you go." The last remark had been made to the wheelhouse. Then he left the compass for the side of the bridge where he could look down the whole length of the ship.

With engines at "slow" and steaming into the weather, the *Hecate* was barely making way through the water. The duty part of the watch had been mustered as "lowerers" and two groups of men held the ropes that would lower the boat to the water. Leaning over the side of the bridge, Murrell looked over the seas ahead, until, seeing a succession of smaller waves, he motioned downward with his hand. Thompson's face, at that distance no more than a white mask without expression, had been turned upwards to the bridge. The Captain watched the boat sink jerkily towards the water as the men eased her down. The davit heads bobbed under her weight.

Thompson's head was turned away and his arm was outstretched. It rose and fell like a musician conducting an orchestra — with seven men's lives depending on his judgment. Murrell realized how Wheeler's absence would increase his own responsibility. Thompson's arm stopped and the white blob of his face was turned inquisitively to the bridge.

Murrell took a long look forward and decided that the next sequence of waves was as good as could be expected. If only Thompson could judge the precise moment the boat should be safely put in the water. He motioned downward with his hand, then, repressing a fever of impatience, walked to the back of the bridge. As he did so, he saw Thompson's hand fall. With a splash the boat was in the water, the oars out, and she was pulling strongly away.

With a sigh of relief the Captain went back to the compass platform. Graves, the gunnery officer, had the afternoon watch. "Boat's clear," Murrell said with a flutter of inward satisfaction that his appreciation of the waves and the position in which he had slipped the boat could hardly have been bettered. "I'll take her;" and down the voice pipe, "Half ahead. Port twenty. Steer one-eight-oh."

As the *Hecate* swung around they could see the boat, small and insignificant in the immensity of the ocean. But very soon after it had left their side it was, when it went down into the trough of a wave, lost to view. Then it would be lifted into sight again. At first they saw only a row of heads, then the oars beating in time, and lastly, as the wave's crest passed beneath it, the whole boat would be seen as it rocked backwards and began its slide down the smooth waveback.

Wheeler was making a pass under the *Antioch's* stern. In a much wider circle Murrell followed him around. It was a great temptation to move in closer, but once he had handed over the party to Wheeler he did not wish to give the appearance of interfering in the attempt to board the *Antioch*. Under no circumstances could he be any help, and the younger officer's feeling of being closely watched might well of itself produce a hasty judgment. In the event, he kept further away than he had intended.

The watchers on the bridge could now see the tanker's lee side. Two sets of boat's falls hung down from the naked davit heads.

28

The lower blocks dipped in the sea as the big ship rolled. From her side a rope ladder with wooden treads hung precariously. It was not easy to make out, even with the glasses, exactly what was happening, and Murrell felt his whole body as much under strain as he thought Wheeler's must be. To watch without being able to help was more strain than doing the job himself.

Someone was on the ladder, was clambering up, was over the rail. Another, and another. It was impossible to put names to the oilskin-clad bundles as they clung precariously to their slender hold. Four men had climbed aboard. Then there was a holdup while watchers held their breath and wondered what delayed the rest of the men in the boat. Men were climbing again, five — six — seven, and the boat was backing away, turning and paddling downwind to where the *Hecate* waited.

Murrell seized the lanyard of the siren. Against the immensity of the ocean the little noise would be cast in defiance. The wind whipped the steam around the funnel as it roared out of the siren's mouth. Although the noise shook the eardrums of those on the bridge, only with luck would it be heard on the *Antioch.* In long and short blasts, the Captain gave the letters D G. Dog George. Damned good. Or, as the naval code had it for these letters, "manoeuvre well executed."

Macmillan, guessing the reason and interpreting the siren's notes as a call to fortitude as much as a gesture of defiance, smiled happily to himself. Until the *Antioch* was ready to be taken in tow, there would be little to see. He thought he might as well go down to his cabin, and walked quietly from the bridge.


As Murrell turned the *Hecate's* bows into the seas, to pick up the whaler he was reminded of his thoughts of the morning. It seemed he was going to have ample opportunity to handle the ship, and for this he was grateful. There were few pleasures more satisfying than the delicate balancing of rudder and engines against wind and waves. It was something real to set against a vague apprehension.

He would like to have pointed out to the doctor that you had to wait for circumstance to call for your specialist skill, but when he turned he found Macmillan gone. The doctor, he thought, was a strange lone wolf. Warm-hearted and friendly, he would pay his uninvited but welcome calls, and then, after administering his mental medicine, as suddenly disappear.

But the whaler was close under the bow and he had other things to think about. At one moment the boat was nearly level with the deck and the next below the black band of the waterline. Slowly Murrell let the *Hecate* creep up until the whaler was under the davits. He saw the falls jerk tight as the boat was hooked on, saw the men on deck begin to haul away. He caught a glimpse of the boat clear of the water, and, thankful that this too had been accomplished, he went back to the compass platform. "Half ahead, starboard fifteen. Steer oh-three-oh." With the boat recovered, he could get the ship under way again, and with U-boats about, no one, neither officers nor men, liked their ship to be stopped in mid-ocean. Fear was measured inversely to the speed of the ship. He said to Graves, "I want to circle the *Antioch* at about a mile." And then, above the noise of a ship at sea, he heard from below the high-pitched shouts of men in trouble and a dull crash he could not explain.

Flinging himself to the back of the bridge, he saw the whaler held only by the after fall. Its bow hung down. A wave catching the boat flung it against the ship's side. The cause of the crashing was more than explained.

Half a ship's length away, and with events moving with a rapidity that no action of his could control, Murrell suddenly found himself again reduced from the master to a mere spectator of the action of others. He could only stand in horrified silence while far below him Gray, the Commissioned Gunner, leaped for the davit head. As the human figure clung to the curved metal that bucked alarmingly as the boat was caught and wrenched by the seas, Murrell saw the flash of the knife that hacked at the lashing. Gray had made his own decision and, fearful that the hanging boat would stave in the thin plating of the destroyer's hull, he was trying to cut her adrift. He saw the cut ends of rope part under the knife. A moment later the boat fell with a splash into the sea and drifted astern.

The Captain turned heavily and went back to the compass platform. The eyes of all those on the bridge were expressionless, both officers and men. None could see a boat — the symbol of safety — lost without feeling a catch in the heart that his own chance of safety had been lessened. From the attitude of the men on deck, Murrell guessed that no man had gone overboard with the boat. That was his only consolation.

"Well, the boat's gone, and even if we could get her she's too battered to be worth picking up. It's fortunate for you that the men in the boat were holding onto the lifelines and you were able to get 'em aboard. Otherwise you'd have had to face a pretty rough Board of Enquiry." Murrell, looking at the dejected Thompson, had to force himself to speak with resignation. He would very much rather have indulged in the luxury of losing his temper. But to have done so would only have weakened still further Thompson's authority in the ship. The order to move, given too early and without sufficient care, had lost them the boat, threatened the lives of the three men in her, and gravely reduced the chance of taking Wheeler and his men off the tanker, should it be necessary to do so. He had to admit that, overlooking the difference in competence between his first lieutenant and the man who stood before him, he had himself, by increasing speed and altering course, made disaster inevitable.

Without the whaler there would be no means of putting more men aboard the *Antioch*. The motor boat was not fitted with slipping gear and, with the ship at sea, could be put in the water only when the weather was perfect. His thoughts were interrupted by Graves' voice. "The tow is signalling, sir."

Dismissing Thompson, Murrell went back to the compass. "Tow?" And somehow he managed a smile. "How nice to be so sure of yourself," he said as he climbed up beside the Officer of the Watch. From the wing of the *Antioch's* bridge a light flickered. The voice of the signalman reading the signal could be heard plainly.

"Preparatory report. Engine room flooded. Fuel-oil tanks port side buckled and leaking. Remainder of hull appears undamaged. Quite impracticable to steam, but tow possible. All cable work will

31

have to be done by hand as winches are electric. Am preparing to tow as arranged. Will signal when ready."

"Yeoman," the Captain called, "we'd better make a signal to *Bruce* and Commander-in-Chief Western Approaches. Let me have a pad, please." He went into the chart house.

He could hear the clack of the shutter of the signal lamp and, without meaning to read it, he did so from habit. It was a private signal from one signalman to another. "What is it like over there?"

Murrell thought he'd like to know what answer was given. Peering through the one little scuttle of the chart house, he could just see the tanker and the little stab of light that winked from the high hump of the bridge. "Flipping awful," the light said, and then was extinguished. Looking at the gray shape through the curtain of rain, Murrell thought the sender was probably right.

Taking a pencil from the shallow tray at the back of the chart table, the Captain wrote, "Consider *Antioch* can be salvaged. Main cargo tanks undamaged. Have party aboard and am preparing to tow. Request early arrival of ocean tug, air cover and surface escort. Time of origin 1502."

## Chapter 4

The *Hecate* steamed around the crippled tanker, her track a square whose sides were each a mile long. Her asdic probed the depths for any U-boats, while her men waited to complete the arduous and unaccustomed job of taking a large vessel in tow.

While she was beam-on to the sea, she rolled wildly and with abandon. Then, when her head was brought to the wind, she curtsied deeply to the waves and buried her bow until the palms of the anchors were slapped by the seas. Reaching the turning point and beam-on again, she would repeat the heavy roll, and the side of the bridge which had previously been sheltered was now exposed to the rain. At the end of that leg the destroyer turned downwind. The seas, passing under her, threw up her stern and buried her bow deeply in the back of the wave that had passed under her. Then the rain would fall almost vertically into the unprotected bridge, and whenever her stern sank into a trough a blast of hot funnel gas would be wafted over the group of men clustered around the standard compass.

At each alteration every man aboard had to readjust his body to the new conditions, and found the change of motion more tiring than if the ship had spent the whole on the worst of the courses. The Captain, viewing the passing hours, had an intense desire to make a questioning signal to the dark shape around which he patrolled. But he could be certain that Wheeler and his men were doing everything possible to ensure that the *Antioch* would be ready before nightfall. A signal would only cause annoyance, and, keeping at the best distance to afford protection against a U-boat, those on the *Hecate* were too far away to see what went on. To hide his own impatience Murrell left the bridge and went down to his sea-cabin. But even there, deprived of the already-hated sight of the *Antioch,* he could find no rest. Wheeler might be another hour, or he could be ready in a minute's time. Murrell wandered into the chart room and, careful not to disturb Masters, who was stretched out on the settee, looked again at the barometer. It was down another tenth. Thinking that the blissfully sleeping navigator was an offense to a man who could not rest, he went back to his own cabin. But whether he could find escape or not, it was imperative to give the impression of being free from care. With purposefulness he settled himself at his desk and took a book from the drawer.

Then, at the same time that he discovered he had not read a word, his ears, preternaturally sharp, heard the faint cry on the deck above his head: *"Antioch* signalling." He went up the ladder as fast as his legs would take him.

A white light flickered from the tanker's bridge. "Watch the splash. I am just going to slip the starboard anchor. Will be ready to tow from starboard cable in fifteen minutes. Suggest you take station on my starboard bow."

Murrell heaved a sigh of relief. With positive action to be taken, the warmth of endeavour would oust the cold tension of waiting. "Very well, Mr. Graves. I'll take her. Tell Mr. Thompson that we'll be passing the towing hawser in fifteen minutes. Have the coxswain at the wheel and see that Mr. Gray is ready with the line-throwing rifle." After the long wait it was very satisfactory indeed to have the chance to handle the ship himself.

A rifle sent the first line over. A heavier rope was tied to the line's end, and then, snaking from the deck along which it had been laid, the big towing hawser crept out. Inch by inch, and foot by foot, it grew to form coupling between the low stern of the destroyer and the towering bow of the tanker. Murrell watched the end disappear jerkily into the cavernous hawse pipe that, freed of its anchor, yawned above them. In his intense interest in a delicate piece of seamanship, the possibility of the enemy interfering had receded from the front of his mind. For the moment the weather was his only foe.

From the bridge Murrell had seen Wheeler's head and shoulders above the deep bulwarks. At the moment of seeing each other they had exchanged waves; but now that any hand movement might be interpreted as a signal, no further acknowledgment of friendship could be made. When the hawser had passed up the pipe, Wheeler's head had been withdrawn and White's appeared in its place. The signalman's hands moved swiftly as he passed a message in that peculiar brand of semaphore which is too fast to be read by anyone other than a fleet signalman.

"Have four shackles of cable ranged on deck and held by slip. Without power on the winch I am unable to let it out slowly. It will come all at once when slip is knocked off. Please go ahead as soon as my hand is dropped." The signalman read the message to the Captain.

"Reply, 'Well done,' " Murrell said and raised his voice: "Mr. Graves. Stand by to go half ahead as soon as I give the order."

Wheeler's head reappeared over the *Antioch's* rail. His hand was raised while his head was turned to watch the men who worked on the tanker's deck. The hand fell. "Half ahead seven-oh revolutions," Murrell ordered. "Steady as you go."

That part of the hawser that had been hauled aboard the *Antioch* ran out of the hawse pipe. Then, with a roar that could be heard on the *Hecate's* bridge, the chain cable followed it. In the widening gap between the ships, the cable poured into the sea like falling shot — and then as suddenly stopped. Seven heads appeared over the tanker's bow to exchange cheerful waves with those of the *Hecate's* crew that were clustered around the after house.

As the distance between the ships widened, the cable that hung from the *Antioch's* bow began to move forward. The destroyer, moving faster, raised the hawser from the waves. It came up streaming, and as it took the strain, water was squeezed from it. The falling drips made a dark and dappled line over the waves.

The destroyer, caught by the stern, was checked. Her screws thrashed the water. Murrell sickened at the sensation. A giant had seized his free-floating ship and tied her up. Like a faithful horse she hung her weight into the work — but the collar bit deep into her master's soul.

When the *Hecate* first took the tow, both ships were lying beam-on to the westerly weather with their bows to the northward, and the tow followed her tug reasonably well. But as soon as Murrell tried to draw her around to an easterly course, the devil entered into the *Antioch*. There was so much disparity in size that the ships were differently affected by the waves that overtook them. The big tanker would yaw violently — first one way, then the other. The *Hecate,* with one propeller stopped and the other churning the water, would struggle desperately to bring her charge back on course. For perhaps a minute the odious craft would tow correctly, before once more she swung away.

"You wouldn't think she wanted us to take her home!" Murrell said to the Yeoman who stood beside him. "Trouble is," he went on, "that with the towing hook right at the stern we can only hold ourselves straight by the power of our engines. Now you can see why a real tug has the towing hook nearly in the middle of her — so she can turn herself this way and that while keeping the tow more or less steady. I'm damned if I know how we're to go on doing this until the tug arrives!"

It was already evident that someone would have to con the ship the whole time. Murrell must first learn to do the job himself and then teach someone else. But first he had to find some position where at the same time he could see the stern of his own ship, the way the hawser grew, and the bow of the *Antioch.* This he could not do from the compass platform, but only from the extreme after end of the bridge on one side or the other. But standing there he would be without shelter of any kind and would have to raise his voice to shout instructions to the Officer of the Watch. It was a position that might be supported for one or two hours — possibly for a whole watch. But it was obviously not one that could be held by one man for a long period of time.

The signalman of the watch came with a signal pad. Rain had made the paper sodden, and the wind could not flutter the leaves. The Yeoman took the pad and held it for Murrell. It was past sunset, the light was failing, the wet paper made the pencilled writing difficult to read, and he dared not take his eyes from the tow. "Read it to me, please," he said.

"Senior Officer 40th Escort Group and *Hecate* from C-in-C W.A.," the Yeoman read. "Weather permitting air cover will be provided during daylight hours from 0800 tomorrow. Regret no surface escorts can be detached from convoy duties. No ocean tug immediately available. *Hecate* is to do her utmost to bring *Antioch* in."

"Hell and damnation!" Murrell exploded. "It's five hundred miles! Five days and ... and — oh hell!" Then, seeing the expression of bewilderment on the Yeoman's face, he stopped. It was a burden he must carry alone. His mind, searching desperately for analogy, found nothing that met his needs. The size of the endeavour appeared devastating.

"It don't seem possible, do it, sir?" his Yeoman, his confidential signalman, said.

A remembered image came to Murrell. "Ever seen an ant trying to get a dead butterfly across a lawn?"

The Yeoman nodded. "Yes, sir."

"We're the bloody ant!" Murrell told him.

Looking aft he saw the tow begin a sheer to port. Raising his voice, he shouted to Masters, who at four o'clock had relieved Graves on watch. "Starboard twenty. Stop starboard engine. One-five-oh revolutions port engine."

The *Hecate's* stern dipped. A blast of funnel gas, hot and sulphurous, set him coughing.

## Chapter 5

When Wheeler struggled up the rope ladder that hung from the *Antioch's* stern there were moments when he thought he might not have the physical strength to make the climb. The force that drove him on was almost entirely fear: not so much the fear of losing his foothold on the rain-slimed wooden slats as the cold dismay of being shown to be inferior to his men. He had been desperately glad to feel Pengelley's hands help him over the rail.

The effort, calling for the extreme of energy, left him clutching the rail. It seemed to him that, with a mind so receptive to the visual image, he would never forget the method or the moment of his arrival. The main deck from which the ladder hung had the boat deck above it, and so the place where he stood was sheltered from the weather. A quietness, more noticeable by reason of a multitude of small noises, hung over the deserted ship.

There were strange clicks, clacks and tappings. Ears that were strained to utmost sensitivity constrained the newcomers to talk in whispers. At the same time, their hushed voices were heard with unnatural clarity.

Pengelley had been the first to go aboard, and Hart the next. Then Wheeler had made the climb, followed by Sibson, Anders, Trotman and White. Now, like trespassers fearing to advance on ground that is not theirs, they stood clustered around the head of the ladder. Wheeler realized that they waited for his lead, as much as the three men in the boat waited for his order to return to the *Hecate*. The expression "all eyes were turned to him" had a new force. It was his first experience of real command. There was no one senior to whom matters could be referred. He was out on a limb by himself, with the others dependent on him. Leaning over the rail, he waved to Richards in the boat.

The whaler backed away, turned in the shelter of the tanker's hull and was soon paddling away downwind to where, in the rain-smoked distance, the destroyer waited. They watched her go in distrustful silence. The tanker rolled heavily, and from somewhere within her there came a loud clang. "Christ!" White's voice was strained. "What's that?" Seeking assurance, the eyes of the six men flickered from one to the other.

With an effort Wheeler said, "They got out in a hurry — something loose. Come on. We'll look at the fo'c'sle."

"Ain't she flipping big." Sibson in wonder spoke softly. "You wouldn't think a thing as big as this could sink."

"That big bastard that blew up beside us — she sank all right," White said, and in the silence that followed, "What was her name?"

*"Tapico,"* Wheeler told him, imparting information just because he knew it and just because he was their officer and had urgent need to impress the fact. "Fourteen thousand tons of high-octane petrol. Come on, let's go and see what the fo'c'sle is like." But the last sentence had not carried the conviction of an order, and no one moved. Wheeler knew he would have to do better than that.

Under the shelter of the deck above they seemed to find protection from more than the weather. Like a covey of partridge shielded by long grass from a passing hawk, there was a blind resistance to any movement.

"She were gone in half a minute!" Pengelley reminded them.

"It wasn't really as long as that," Wheeler said. "The visual impressions pass so rapidly across the retina of the eye that the brain assumes they must have taken longer than in fact they did. The official report gave the time as fifteen seconds." He was passing on a dictum of Macmillan's. Memory, speeded by anxiety, had carried him back to a discussion in the *Hecate's* wardroom. And that battened-down and stale-aired wardroom that smelled of damp sea clothes, of their last meal, and of musty tobacco, where the chairs were littered with half-torn periodicals and the linoleum slimed with condensation, now seemed a wholly desirable place in which to be. At the moment Wheeler would have given a great deal to have transferred himself from the one place to the other.

"Fifteen seconds, nor thirty, don't make that much difference," Hart said.

"Just long enough to holler out." Pengelley's voice was taut.

"The howling was the worst part of it." White's eyes swept around the group. He was the youngest there and looked it. "I won't never forget it!"

"There was a full seventy of them — only seven of us. You'd not hear a squeak," Hart told him.

Anders, the big slow man, turned on them a face contorted with rage. "You silly flipping bastards, what the hell are you playing at? Standing here like a lot of flipping schoolgirls on a railway platform. For Christ's sake, let's get doing something."

"Anders is right." Wheeler started to move forward. And to Hart: "Get the men mustered on the fo'c'sle."

But Hart was looking over the side towards the destroyer. "They've got the whaler, sir," he said. Wheeler was glad to hear the term "sir" reappear in speech. It promised a return to normality.

"Like hell they have!" Pengelley said. "Oh, for Christ's sake . . . !"

In stricken silence the seven men watched the whaler's bow fall down as the destroyer turned away. With awe in his voice Wheeler said, "They'll lose her!"

"They have — and so have we," Pengelley said. "Anyway, after that banging-about she wouldn't carry a crew of mice."

"How will we get off?" White asked.

"Unless you're J. C. Himself, an' can walk across the waters, you'll swim for it!" By sacrilege Pengelley lashed out at both himself and White. "Ain't you never seen a chap pulled out of the 'oggin? Ain't you never seen what the barnacles does to his hands as he tries to keep hisself off the ship's bottom?"

"Nonsense," Wheeler snapped, trying to rally morale. "They'll let a Carley Float down to us on a line."

"Oh, sir." Pengelley, older than the others and a proven seaman, could challenge his officer. "Think of the weather side of this ship at the moment. The seas be splashing up against it like a southerly gale on Plymouth Breakwater. You'd never get down to a raft that side. The boats here what didn't get away are burnt to cinders. And you can't float a raft upwind, not however hard you try. Unless another escort turns up with a boat — it's swimming for us if we wants to get off."

"Then we'll stay here until we're towed in."

"God help us, sir. Not that long!" Hart exclaimed.

Wheeler, ignoring the remark, said, "Hart. Get the men mustered on the fo'c'sle." He began to make his way toward the bows. The others, after a moment's pause, followed him.

Reaching the end of the after superstructure, they stood in a close group. Beyond the rain-swept deck, squared by the tank tops and crossed by pipes, was the centre island of the bridge. There were three decks to the structure, many portholes and half a dozen doors. "Ruddy rabbit warren." Trotman spoke their thoughts.

"It don't seem as deserted as it should," White answered. "Feels like someone's watching you. Maybe there is someone left aboard."

"Nonsense," Wheeler told them. "If there was, he'd have seen us."

"Not if he'd any sense," Sibson answered. "He'd have found hisself some liquor and got hisself dead drunk."

Wheeler, noticing the absence of the usual "sir," realized again the tenuous hold of command over men, and knew that only by his own efforts would he be able to turn the stripes on his arm into real authority.

Hart held up his bundle. "What are we going to do with these?"

"Put them inside one of those doors in the bridge. They'll keep dry there." Wheeler, leaning on the wind, led the way across the deck and canted his head against the rain. He found a door on the lee side of the bridge. It opened into a passage. They piled their bundles inside.

"What if there was someone, and he snitched them while we're away?" White asked.

"Don't be more of a fool than you need," Hart said without impatience.

Leaving the shelter of the bridge, they went along the foredeck, pausing and stumbling with the unfamiliar roll of the larger vessel, becoming spread out until they looked like so many crows making their way home against a winter wind. One by one they climbed the iron ladder to the fo'c'sle head.

41

The next two hours were entirely employed in physical labour of the most strenuous kind. And Wheeler was glad of the chance to impose the discipline of thought and action to which they had all been trained. The nearness of the destroyer had given them a sense of security, and even the loss of the whaler came to be no more than a part of the general uncertainty.

When the tow had been fixed Wheeler led his men up to the wheelhouse. There they found emergency oil lights and wooden shutters to blank off the bridge windows. It had been night when the Greeks had left her, and so they had only to light the lanterns, which fortunately had been kept filled. After the cramped and crowded quarters of a destroyer, the tanker's wheelhouse appeared a vast and barren place. "It's as big as a bloody dance hall," Hart said as he looked around.

"We'll turn it into a mess deck for the lot of us," Wheeler told him. "While White keeps signal watch, we'll hunt in pairs for what we want. Hart and Sibson, see what you can find out about the galley — and if there's any fuel to light it with. Pengelley and Trotman, have a look round the fo'c'sle and see if you can find the lamp room. Bring back two more oil lamps and a drum of oil. Anders, come with me and we'll have a scout round the officers' cabins and collect some bedding."

As he went down the interior ladder, torch in hand, he wondered why he had sent them in pairs. Partly to solve the age-old problem of preventing men from thinking about their trials by keeping them employed, but more for mutual support. An aura of fear hung over the lifeless ship and could not be dispelled by any appeal to logic. Within the dark, deserted hull that creaked and groaned continually and was so very empty, he admitted to a strong disinclination to be alone.

In the captain's cabin the wavering beam of his torch lit bedclothes hanging over the bunkboard. The owner had evidently been in his bunk when the ship was struck. A sideboard, the doors of which they forced, contained a number of tinned delicacies. On its top were deep racks for holding wine bottles, and a large wooden box more than half full of cigarettes. Wheeler raised the lid and sniffed. "Not bad," he said to his companion. "We can come back for them afterwards. Let's have this bed for the first."

Anders, gathering the mattress and blankets in his great arms, dumped the lot in the alley way. They carried the bedding from the two cabins on the opposite side of the ship, and on the deck below found three more cabins and the officers' dining saloon. Here they paused in their bed collecting to look at the pantry, which yielded some tins of milk, a fine ham that had hardly been touched, and a variety of pickles.

"We want one more mattress. I expect the engineers will have slept aft over the engines. Let's go and look." Wheeler led the way along the open well deck. By leaning over the ship's side he could just make out the *Hecate,* a dim blur ahead. The *Antioch* was not towing well, but there was nothing he could do about it. He went on into the after part of the ship with Anders, like a great dog, at his heels. Here the atmosphere was decidedly threatening. The air had a strange smell, compounded of oil, sea water, and the acrid smell of recently burned paintwork. Within the flooded engine room the sea slopped and gurgled eerily. In the darkness the two men paused to clip the door through which they had just come. Wheeler, turning the clips, was aware of Anders' sudden start and intake of breath. At the other end of the alley way — an impossible distance away — a gentle fluorescence wavered and danced and became ever so slightly brighter.

Wheeler felt the sudden clutch of the big man's hand on his arm, a grip so fierce that he too came near crying out. For, in addition to the pain of the grip, he had felt the skin of his neck tingle and stretch as his hair stood on end.

"Christ save us!" Anders whispered.

"For God's sake, don't be a fool," Wheeler gasped, "and let go of my arm. It's only the others looking for the galley!"

But the sensation had been far from pleasant, and the knowledge of the stolid Anders' nearness to panic was deeply disturbing. So much so that a real visitation of the supernatural would almost have been preferable to the self-knowledge and sheepishness that the incident had left behind.

Back in the wheelhouse with their bundles, they found the others already arrived. Compared with the rest of the ship, the place already appeared a haven of sanity, and, as the seven mattresses were unrolled and the blankets shared out, it rapidly acquired a lived-in aspect. Pengelley and Trotman had returned with two more lights, a can of oil and a funnel. Hart and Sibson had found the galley, and although it was fired by oil it would not work without electricity for the fans. Hart, however, thought that with a little work he could make it burn wood. They had also found the storeroom, which had tinned meat enough and quite a supply of macaroni. Of bread they'd only found a few rolls.

Wheeler, as he wound and set the clock that was fixed to the bulkhead behind the now-useless wheel, felt that in restarting the visual flow of time he was helping the return to something like an ordinary life. Certainly the gloom was reduced. "We might be a lot worse off," he said. "But there's one thing you've got to remember. The enemy isn't the only agent that can set fire to this lot and fry us all. You *must* not smoke except on this bridge — and even then you'll have to stub out your cigarettes before you go on deck. Now about watches. There are six of you with White, but he'll be needed for signalling. Yes, what is it, Sibson?"

"Watches? What the hell do we want to stand watches for? We can't do nothing by night."

"But we got to have watches!" Hart said. "We're a ship, aren't we?"

"Bloody fine ship's company we are," Sibson said. "Work all the bloody day, and hang about half the flipping night looking at something we can't do nothing about."

Wheeler saw Sibson's eyes make a quick appraisal of possible support. There was again a moment of suspense while all, and most particularly Sibson, waited for his own next words. "You'll stand your watch along with the others," Wheeler told him.

"That's right," Hart said, "we can't sit round on our fannies doing now't!"

Wheeler sensed that Hart carried the others with him — but only just. In this new situation, however much they might wish for the luxury of spending all night on a mattress, they had also an instinctive need to continue the routine.

Sibson bowed to the weight of general opinion, but left no doubt of his own conviction. "Lot of bloody nonsense!" He spoke with truculence and turned away.

Wheeler, hoping that usage would make the point for him, hurried on: "White will be a dayman. The rest of us will keep watch in pairs. We might as well stick to the couples in which we have already hunted. That will put us in three watches. Anders and I will take the Second Dog. Pengelley and Hart can toss for which pair has the First Watch. The losers will have the Middle. Anders and I get the morning. Come on, Anders, we'll go out and relieve White now." He wanted to keep Anders with him and as much as he could away from the others. He kept telling himself that he had not been frightened along with Anders, but with whatever conviction he spoke he didn't seem to be hearing it very plainly. The words were thin as cellophane and cast no shadow on the mind.

With Anders on one wing of the bridge and himself forty feet away on the other, Wheeler felt a reaction from the keyed-up excitement of the past six hours. At the age of twenty-four he was still young enough for his first thoughts on boarding a derelict in the middle of the Atlantic to have been brightened by memories of adventure stories from boyhood. It was not until he was alone in the rain-laden dark that the thought of what the enemy might do came home to him. Then the more he thought of the excellent target that the slow-moving ships would make, the more queasy his stomach felt.

For comfort he told himself that the weather which made towing so difficult had reduced visibility to the point where any encounter would be in the nature of a collision. But they were five hundred — or possibly by that time only four hundred and ninety — miles from home. He had no knowledge of when a tug would come to their assistance, and no idea how they were going to be disembarked from their temporary home.

Next, he wondered if Sibson was going to cause trouble. He had perhaps been too intent on choosing strength without giving sufficient care to character. It was odd how distinctly the vision returned of his first few moments aboard the *Antioch*. It was almost as if they had been painted, framed and hung in his room at home so that he would see the picture each morning when he woke. What an eerie sensation he had experienced with Anders in the alley way.

On his next leave he really must build the rockery he'd promised his mother he'd make. But then there was Anne. Anne was a problem.

The business of courting Anne took time and was surely more important than a rockery. Just how important was it? Even to consider something as definite as marriage in his present precarious position seemed to be tempting fate. He had to admit that he'd been holding back, waiting until he was quite sure. And tonight for the first time, he was. As long as he'd felt sure of his return, he'd felt the question was one that could be left to find its own answer. But now he wanted desperately to speak to her, to ask her to marry him — and soon: as soon as arrangements could be made. Supposing she wouldn't agree?

The thought brought an urgency that he'd not known before, and all at once he was frightened of losing his life before ever he'd had the chance to ask her. If he got ashore again, he'd not hesitate. In the meantime he'd have to take care. His fingers, searching inside his duffel-coat, felt for the comforting band of his inflatable life jacket. Self-consciously he inflated it a little — just in case: in case there was time to get out.

"Pengelley relieving, sir." The voice, sounding unexpectedly beside him, made him jump. He hoped the Leading Seaman did not think he'd been asleep on watch. "Good Lord, I didn't know it was eight bells already!"

Pengelley laughed. "Strange how a watch goes faster when there's nothing at all to see or do."

"I've nothing to turn over to you," Wheeler said. *"Hecate* has still got the tow. Even if it looks as if we're not moving — I reckon we're making about four knots. The wind is strong enough to blow the surface water along with it, so our own speed looks that much lower. Goodnight, Pengelley."

## Chapter 6

To Murrell, on the *Hecate's* bridge, the slowly deepening night in one way increased, but in another eased, the tension. When he could see neither the *Antioch's* wild yaws nor the surge of the hawser that connected the two ships, he had just that amount less to worry about. He no longer strained his eyes to detect the first slight movement of the *Antioch's* masts, in an endeavour to anticipate her next cavort, but waited until the dark mass of her hull had swung considerably one way or the other before he made any alteration in his own ship's engines or rudder.

During daylight his orders to the Officer of the Watch had been almost continuous. With the night they were made far less frequently. Gray, the Commissioned Gunner, had fitted up a telephone and chest pad, and now the Officer of the Watch had earphones under the hood of his duffel-coat, and the Captain a mouthpiece strapped to his chest. The wire trailing across the deck was a nuisance and easily became entangled with his feet. He had to remember that if he turned one way he must turn back the other, but at least he had not to shout his orders.

A dark shape appeared beside him. "Your medical adviser," the doctor announced his identity.

"That remark sounds a little ominous. Do you want to feel my pulse, or give me a pill?"

"I was just interested to see how long you could stand it." In the dark the doctor interpreted the silence that greeted his remark as a shrug of the shoulders.

"Starboard twenty. Slow starboard," the Captain announced into the mouthpiece.

"So you think you can go on doing that for the next five days?"

"I hope it won't be as long as that," Murrell said.

"But it may be," the doctor answered. "What then?"

"Look, Doc, I've bloody well got to try." Murrell was made vehement by his own fear of the outcome.

"Well, speaking as your medical gentleman, I'll tell you here and now that you bloody well can't."

"Mahomet and the Mountain," the Captain murmured as he raised his binoculars to peer into the murk astern. Then he bent his head. "Midships. Half ahead together."

"A false analogy — and Mahomet was not a sailor."

"But seriously, Doctor, what else can I do? You don't think I like this, do you? just between you and me, I'm hating it."

"You certainly can't do it all the time, and you won't."

"I could arrest you for interfering," the Captain remarked conversationally.

"I could certify you as insane. That would fix you."

"Good Lord! Could you?"

"If you go on like this, I'll probably have to."

"Port ten," the Captain ordered, while he thought over the doctor's remark. Then, "So what?"

"You've got to teach someone else."

"Have you thought who? You saw the mess Thompson made this afternoon. Wheeler could have done this. I've got to have officers of the watch. The ship must go on — the tow is not the only thing. Once the weather clears, the enemy won't miss their chance."

"How about me?" Macmillan asked.

"You?"

"I may not be an executive officer, but I've played about with boats since I was a child. Count it my misfortune to be a medico — that's all. I don't for one moment say I'll do it as well as you do, and sooner or later I'll probably part the tow. We'll just have to accept that. Do be reasonable. The two of us may get her in. You can't possibly do it alone."

There was a long silence while the Captain pondered the suggestion. He knew that the doctor's contention was reasonable, but found some difficulty in adjusting himself to the idea of sharing his task with a surgeon. He had to admit that another twenty-four hours would be about the limit of his physical endurance. After that his efficiency would drop so rapidly that an alternative would be

48

essential. As he had said to Macmillan, there was not only the question of the tow; he must keep some part of his brain to deal with the enemy when the latter should put in an appearance.

There had been many occasions when he had looked into a future in which there had appeared no relief for whatever trouble loomed largest; but then, as with gales, he had found that, provided he dug his toes in, the trouble would disappear — or the gale blow itself out. He was not strong enough to manage without accepting this offer, and he had to take it with gratitude. That would not be difficult, for whatever his spirit, his body already longed for the relaxation of his cabin.

"Thank you, Doctor," he said to the figure beside him, and began to divest himself of the harness that held the mouthpiece to his chest.. "I'll stay with you for half an hour."

"I hoped you'd do that," Macmillan said. "I've told Kirby to have your dinner in your sea-cabin at eight o'clock. I had mine before I came up."

"The hell you have!" Murrell exclaimed. "What determined chaps you medicos are."

"And don't we need to be! Now begin to teach me my new trade of tug-master."


In the warmth and seclusion of his own sea-cabin there was much to suggest that his *Hecate* was in her normal station astern of the convoy. Only the peculiarly heavy feel of the ship was a continual reminder of her present unnatural task.

Until he had sat down before his dinner, Murrell had not realized how hungry he was. Relaxed, he began to think — and at once saw again the force of the doctor's words. He had been so absorbed in conning the ship that he had been guilty of overlooking obvious and dangerous facts. Their asdic could be heard at a very considerable distance by a German hydrophone operator. In the present bad visibility, a U-boat could only sight a ship if it were less than a mile away. To stop the asdic transmissions was to reduce the chance of the enemy finding them. He picked up the telephone to the bridge. Thompson's voice answered him.

49

"Thompson, you'd better stop the asdic transmissions. If a U-boat wants to attack us in this weather he'll come in on the surface, and then the radar should detect him." Murrell waited for Thompson's acknowledgment and then replaced the handset.

Thank Heaven that in February, 1943, they had radar, and the German U-boats had not. If the Radar Office did pick up an echo, he'd have to slip the tow. Gray was standing by in the stern to knock off the slip if it were necessary. Now that he had the doctor to relieve him he could plan the necessary alteration in his ship's routine. In his own tiredness he had overlooked Gray. To give the gunner relief, the Second Officer of the Watch could be sent aft, for either the doctor or he would be conning the ship. The pieces of the puzzle were fitting into place. He had to admit that despite the strange sensation of fear there was intense interest in all the changes that the *Antioch* had brought with her.

The sense of fear was difficult to define. The word had many connotations, and the feeling many shapes. He thought that he had already met a number of these, but now seemed to recognize a new one. Unlike cowardice, an act, fear was an acceptable emotion which, at its lowest valuation, made you face facts and take precautions. When matched against the enemy you threw into the scales your character and your background: all the ties of family, school and naval tradition were there to help you. And you had many things with which to help yourself: your weapons, your speed, and the efficiency of your men. All could be used to thrust at the enemy's weakness or parry his strength — and if you lost, it just meant that you were the weaker at that particular place and time.

The *Hecate* and *Antioch* tied together were a target in the full sense of the word. Anything the enemy sent would have the initiative, and, however great their own endeavours, it did not appear they could succeed without a great measure of luck. To be so dependent on uncertain chance was the negation of good seamanship. It seemed to reduce the whole sorry business to the spin of a coin, and made the effort appear worthless. Perhaps this was the kernel of the new fear: to work for something where the God-given excess of zeal over mere duty could be expected to make little difference.

At least that was something concrete you could pray God to give you. To ask Him to interest Himself in the immediate affairs of the *Antioch* seemed presumptuous when quite likely one of the enemy would be praying that the tanker would be sunk; "Render therefore to Caesar the things that are Caesar's; and unto God the things that are God's." The greater matter, the final outcome of the war, might possibly be God's concern. But could you separate a part from the whole? Man made evil look so different, depending on the side he was on. Come to think of it, man had, even with His help, never really succeeded in coming to terms with evil, nor even drawn its outlines with certitude. So where was he, Murrell, in this shifting scene? Was it not just his duty to do his utmost to get the tanker in? Without consideration of the major issues? Anyway, it was time to go up and see how the doctor was managing. But in the effort to think of something other than the immediate problems of ships and sea, he had found some refreshment.

He went into the chart room to have another look at the barometer.

Moving carefully, so that he should not disturb the Navigator, the Captain looked at the mercury. There had been no further fall. He went up to see Macmillan. If all should be well with the doctor, he'd have a couple of hours' sleep before midnight. Then he would take over the con until four in the morning.


The winter dawn came sluggishly, and in no particular direction was it lighter than anywhere else; and, as a sad apology for sunrise, the rain became visible again. The long narrow pencil of the ship that had, during the night, been a darker tone of black than the sea around her had now imperceptibly changed until she was lighter in colour than the seas. In this transformation there had been a time when the tones of ship and sea had been the same. Then, in spite of the driving rain, she had for a moment achieved a mantle of almost ethereal beauty — but it was short-lived, and, as so frequently happens, the rain was heavier with the coming of dawn.

But there were cups of hot "kai" being handed around by the bosun's mate, and life was stirring once more. "Tow signalling," the doctor called.

Murrell, who after three hours' sleep had come on deck at seven o'clock, joined the doctor. Astern of them, seeming to loom larger as her outline was blurred by the driving rain, the big tanker slid awkwardly over the waves, and as she yawed she presented a view first down one side and then down the other. From the centre of her bridge the light flickered, as, shining through the rain, it gathered an added nimbus. It was only natural that Wheeler should wish to break the silence of the night watches as soon as daylight had come.

"Please let me have recipe for cooking macaroni," the signal started. "Have plenty of meat, but no other starch food. Would appreciate daily cookery signal."

The Navigator passed them. "The glass is rising, sir," Masters said.

" 'Morning, Pilot. I rather expected so. This heavier rain suggests a break in the cloud. Wind'll fly north of west when it clears. I'm going down to get my breakfast — be up at eight to relieve you, Doctor. Anyway, Wheeler and his lads are all right if their first interest is food."

Murrell began to descend the ladder. He was halfway down when a sea caught the ship. She was flung sideways, and he had to grasp the ladder firmly to avoid being thrown to the deck below. As she hung poised on the wave he felt her stern drawn back by the tow as if part of his own body had been caught. And then suddenly she was free — kicking her heels like a young colt as she bounded over the seas.

"Tow parted!" He heard the shout which confirmed what his body had already told him.


It was only too true. Murrell, clinging to the standard compass, looked across the heaving waters to the tanker which, released from its tow, was now turning to lie once more broadside on to the seas. Her bows were towards the *Hecate* as the latter swung in a broad circle, and it could be seen that from her starboard hawse pipe the cable hung straight into the sea.

Already the Yeoman, whose ability to appear whenever anything occurred was only matched by the speed of his departure as soon as matters became normal once more, had rejoined his captain. "Send to *Antioch,*" Murrell told him: "Consider tow has parted at extreme end of your cable. Am recovering hawser now while steaming slowly around you. Can you recover . your cable?"

The Captain turned to Thompson. "Commence normal asdic sweep." Then the *Antioch* was signalling back. "To *Hecate:* Agree your diagnosis. Regret unable to recover cable in anything like reasonable time. Submit we recommence tow with port cable. Can probably improve slightly on yesterday's time for preparation. Starboard cable can be recovered at leisure."

The Captain was dictating the signals direct to the Yeoman at the light, a procedure which saved time; and as each knew the other so intimately it was highly satisfactory. "Don't be downhearted. With drift and tow you are nearly a hundred miles nearer home than this time yesterday. Consider weather will clear and wind shift to northwest. Some bloody fool — erase--erase — erase. We have hawser foul of port propeller. Continue preparation while I clear myself."

## Chapter 7

Hans Edelmann, co-pilot of the big four-engined Focke-Wulf aircraft, leaned forward to catch his captain's words. "What did you say?" he asked.

"We ought to meet that cold front soon," Richter repeated.

"Might as well have stayed comfortably in Bordeaux as be flying around the Atlantic in this weather," Edelmann answered. "I only wish the Officers of the Staff had to come out on some of these missions!"

"It is clearing a little now — let's go down and look at the waves," the Captain said.

"Not too close — I hate swimming." His co-pilot grinned without humour.

Slowly the big plane lost height. The drone of its engines was absorbed in the immensity of the sky, and in the driving rain it seemed to have no more substance than a shadow.

The two German officers peered inquisitively through the perspex windows and glanced at the altimeter with apprehension.

"Two hundred," Edelmann told his captain. The plane, with engines eased, continued its slow descent.

"Soon we must see something," Richter grumbled, and prayed the altimeter was correctly set, "even if it's only a wavetop. Otherwise, as you say, we might as well have stayed at home."

But Edelmann was not listening. With his gloved hand he rubbed at the perspex and peered out. *"Herr Kapitän — Herr Kapitän!* A big tanker. Do you see her?"

Peering forward, Richter pulled the joy stick slightly towards him. The thrum of the engines rose steadily and increased as the throttles were opened. "Yes. I see her — and an escort circling."

"You will attack, *Herr Kapitän?"*

"No. We are of the Reconnaissance Wing. In this weather one cannot tell who would win. We'd have no time to set the bombsights and could only attack from such a low altitude that we'd be sure to be hit ourselves. I will report the position. It is for our U-boats, of whose great deeds one is sick of hearing, to deal with that tanker — and the escort."

The shadow, which had not been seen in either ship because both crews were too busy with their own troubles, winged away to the eastward.


U-boat 506 was virtually hove-to. On the ninth of February, two nights before, she had executed a raid on an eastbound convoy and had secured — so she claimed — the obvious jackpot by torpedoing the big tanker that had been in the centre. Slipping between two escorts, running on her diesels, she had dodged between the ships of the convoy, and then, her mission accomplished, had dived deep and escaped.

It was her commanding officer's first patrol as captain, and the tanker his first victim. He had, not without reason, been pleased with himself: a condition that came easily to the inexperienced in the moment of apparent victory.

Lying in his bunk, Korvetenkapitän Willi Lachmann reread a letter from his wife Magda. She wanted to know why he had not had leave for so long. He thought he had explained a hundred times that he'd had to stay about in Lorient, keeping himself before the notice of people that mattered, people who could assure his promotion. It had taken time, and now that at last he had a boat of his own he supposed it would be three months at least before he could hope for leave. But the tanker had been a good start! Possibly his name had already been mentioned on the wireless or in the newspapers and Magda would have learned of his success. He hoped so. Her continual carping about leave in every letter was becoming an annoyance.

He must get up and start to write his first report, and he would have to write it carefully. So much could depend on the way a report was written. And even when, at the end of the war, the records of the British Admiralty were in their hands, there'd be no corresponding report from the two escorts he'd so cleverly eluded. It would be a good and heartening tale. He had never really believed in the wonder-weapon the Allied Navies were supposed to have. Lack of decision on the part of other U-boat captains was the real reason for the recent heavy U-boat losses. Had he not proved it two nights before when, at "reduced buoyancy," with no more than the dark speck of his conning tower showing above the black waves, he'd slipped between two escorts that had been plainly visible to him?

"Herr Kapitän." A voice disturbed this pleasurable reverie, and a hand parted the curtain that hung before his bunk to give the only extra privacy that a U-boat captain knew. Turning on his side, Lachmann saw the narrow hatchet face of Kleist, the signalman, peer through the slit.

"What is it?" Lachmann demanded shortly, annoyed without reason at having his seclusion disturbed.

"A signal for us, Herr Kapitän. From U-boat Command, Lorient."

"Give it me," the Kapitän said as he took the signal, from the man's hand.

Lachmann read it. He read it through again carefully. "Very well," he said. But he did not hand it back, as normally he would have done. He waited, lying on the bunk, while the hot flush of hurt pride crept over his body. He waited until he heard Kleist's feet move away and then, steeling himself, he read the signal a third time.

"U-boat 506 from U-boat Command, Lorient. Reconnaissance aircraft reports damaged 15,000-ton tanker in position 54° 10' North 21° 19' West at 0835 this morning the 11th, accompanied by destroyer escort. As no other attacks have been carried out in the area this vessel is assumed to be tanker claimed sunk by you on the 9th. Position indicates that ship can steam. You are to close the position and sink her. Repeat sink her. Your attention is drawn to my Standing Orders numbers 31 and 46."

Setting the thin sheet of paper delicately on the edge of the bunk, Lachmann raised his hand to the shelf above his head, where a thin official volume rubbed shoulders with his other literature. Taking this down, he thumbed the pages carefully. Order 25, 28. He turned the page and came to Order 31.

"Commanding officers are, when they have penetrated the escort screen, to force home their attacks with the greatest determination. Inside the convoy and on the surface, even though the merchant ships are plainly visible, U-boats are very difficult to see in darkness. At important targets a spread of torpedoes is always to be fired, and the enemy is to be closed until all possibility of a miss is eliminated."

Number 46, when he reached it, was even worse. "Commanding officers are at all times to avoid making false claims. These are not only misleading, but react unfavourably on the officer concerned."

It took Lachmann some few minutes to recover. Then he swung his legs from the bunk and, slipping on his coat, went out into the narrow central gangway and turned aft towards the control room. Gessner, the Navigator, was bending over the chart table. He stood back expectantly when he saw the Kapitän beside him.

Lachmann thought quickly. Everyone in the boat would know that a signal had been addressed to U-506. In the close confines of a U-boat's hull everyone always knew everything that went on. But he had no wish that the exact wording should be known, and the paper now lay crumpled in his own pocket. In the shock, his mind had forgotten the exact position. But he knew that it must be some considerable way to the eastward of his present position, for since his attack — abortive, it now seemed — he had been steaming slowly to the west. Surreptitiously he slid the signal from his pocket and glanced at it. "Lay me off a position 54° 10' North 21° 19' West," he ordered. There was a roughness in his voice that sent the Navigator to his work in a hurry. When the position had been marked, the Navigator stood back.

"How many miles?" Lachmann took a pair of dividers; a moment's work, and he threw the instrument back into the tray. "Zum Teufel! It is one hundred and thirty-eight miles — and 21° 19' West. The British aircraft come as far as 22° West. It means going into the area they cover. And even if she is steaming slowly, she will be east of 20° West before we get there."

"What is it, Herr Kapitän?" Gessner asked.

"A damaged tanker with a destroyer escort. They ask us to repeat our performance." With this mixture of truth and half-truth Gessner must be content. The Kapitän was not going to put the signal on the file. He could, he hoped, trust Kleist, who as a signalman might be supposed to be a confidential servant. But this crew had been together so long that they had developed a herd instinct of their own. Ever since he had taken over from Weissmüller they had persisted in treating him as an interloper. Again, at the thought that every U-boat at sea would have read the unfortunate signal he felt the hot blood rush to the extremities of his body. Other commanding officers would be laughing over it. But there was one man he knew who would not laugh — the Admiral. "What is the course to the position?" he asked, tight-lipped, controlling himself, for whatever happened appearances must be maintained.

"Oh-eight-five degrees, Herr Kapitän," Gessner told him.

"Bring her round to that. Speed fifteen knots."

"Jawohl, Herr Kapitän."

The diesels, that at cruising speed had been making a gentle tap-tap, increased their noise to a shattering roar as the throttles of the powerful engines were opened. The boat, which had been plunging gently with her bow to the westerly weather, shuddered, and, as she turned her side to the waves, rolled heavily. Then, as her head turned downwind to the opposite course, she began a long series of swoops. For a time, riding the crest of the seas, she ran steadily. Then her stern would dip until, overtaken by the next sea, she would pause; to leap forward once more while white water creamed on either side of the conning tower and her wake stretched out behind her — a long undulating ribbon of white laid over the gray sea.

Her men may have sniggered at the signal that their new captain had that morning received. For Kleist had told his friends the purport of the message. But they were careful only to laugh silently and when his back was turned. For all her captain's lack of experience, a savage hound had been laid on to the quarry, with the very efficient U-boat Command to whip it on.

58

## Chapter 8

"I don't believe the cable is around a propeller," Murrell said to Gray as they leaned over the rail and looked at the chain that led straight down into the water. "I think it's foul of the rudder, which makes it better in one way — but worse in another. We've two propellers, and could go home on one alone. We've only one rudder! How in hell's name did she manage to do it?"

"It happened just as she turned into the wind," Gray told him. "She'd very little way on her, and that big wave we hit stopped her nearly dead. As she went over it, her stern came clean out of the water. She must have slapped it down on top of the cable and there we were with an obvious foul. So I telephoned the bridge."

The Engineer Officer joined them. He was a wizened little man who came from Tyneside, where his family had been shipyard workers for generations. He loved machinery in motion more than anything else on earth — certainly more than himself. Under his care the engines never gave a moment's trouble, and Murrell had come to rely on their efficiency as something immutable — a faith touching reverence for the divine. The "Chief," as he overheard the other two, said, "It's easy enough to find out which is fouled. I'll go down to the tiller flat and work the steering engine from there. I'll know at once if there's anything fouling the rudder." He went to the hatch and disappeared down it.

Murrell said, "Let's suppose it is the rudder, and think what we're going to do about it."

A sailor, interrupting, said, "The bridge wants you on the telephone, sir." Gray waited alone. Then Murrell came back. "Our aircraft has shown up," he told Gray. "I must say, that is a relief — especially when both ships are stopped in mid-Atlantic." Involuntarily, as if he sought respite from worry, his hand was raised to brush his forehead. "If it is the rudder," he said, "it can't be more than a bight of the cable caught on the blade. If we could get a wire onto the cable below the rudder, we ought to be able to lift it clear."

"There's only thirty foot of cable before the rope hawser," Gray told him. "The shallow-water diving gear should let a man go down below the ship's bottom."

"In this weather?" Murrell's tone suggested his incredulity.

"I don't see why not, sir. He'd have the cable to get a grip of."

"It'll be bloody cold in the water," Murrell told him.

"I'm prepared to have a try, sir."

"I don't know," Murrell answered. "I don't know at all. I'm no diving expert, but I'd say any man who went down there in this sea would be battered to death against the ship's hull."

The Engineer rejoined them. "Well, Chief?" Murrell asked.

"It's the rudder right enough, sir — and not jammed too tight either. I reckon, by the position of the scrapings I can hear, that the cable is over the forward half of the blade."

"If we could recover the main length of hawser to relieve the weight — and then knock off this slip, the short end might fall clear?" Murrell suggested hopefully.

The Engineer shook his head. "I reckon she's too tight to do that. She'll need a good tug to jog her free. We've got to get a line onto her somehow."

"Then there's nothing for it but to dive," Gray said.

"I don't like it," Murrell told them.

"There's this much about it," the Engineer said, "you won't tow *that* another mile unless you do." He jerked his thumb in the direction of the rain-soaked tanker.

"We can't get on towing until we clear it." Gray restated the obvious.

Murrell, who hated more than anything else being put in the position of having to order men to do what he knew himself incapable of, had to accept the inevitable. "How long will it take to get the diving gear ready?" he asked.

"It'll be half an hour before I can go over the side," Gray told him.

"Then I'll be very grateful if you'll try. But I won't be here when you do. Telephone the bridge when you're ready." Balancing his distaste for risking one brave man against his fear for them all, he made his way forward — and found the balance to hang very level.

When Murrell had climbed back to the bridge, he looked around. The rain clouds were breaking. What had been a continuous gray layer had become a wind-torn mass of dark and leaning shapes against a background that was lighter. The *Antioch,* rolling mightily in the beam sea, showed with greater clarity than before. The colour of the sea had changed from gray to green.

"Barometer's up another tenth, sir. We'll have the clearing within an hour." Masters' tone was one of suggestion.

"We would," Murrell snapped. "We bloody well would!"

And then, apologetic: "Just when we'd most prefer to have remained hidden behind a nice gray curtain of rain, the bloody weather clears. It's enough to make a cow eat meat." He paused, conscious of food and his emptiness. "That reminds me — I'll go down and have my cold breakfast."

Until his mention of eating he had been quite prepared to overlook his lack of a meal. But now he had drawn his own attention to it, he found himself ravenously hungry.

"The aircraft," Masters told him, "has asked if we've any special orders."

For a moment the Captain thought, then: "Yes. Tell him to carry out circular patrols at a radius of alternately two and ten miles." When he was halfway down the companionway, he stopped and shouted to Masters, "Tell him we are very pleased to see him," and "It's nice to know that the staff ashore have not forgotten us."

In his cabin he saw at once that Kirby had made the bunk and tidied the place. It was, he thought, on such very small matters that morale depended. He would have to bear in mind that, whatever happened, the ship's routine must go on. In some circumstances the sight of a neatly folded blanket could be worth a couple of hours of rest. Kirby had jammed his breakfast against the steam radiator. It was somewhat dried, but still edible. He set it on the table and began to eat.

He was drinking his coffee when Masters telephoned from the bridge. "Gray says he's ready to dive, sir."

61

"If there's no reason for my coming up," Murrell said, "I'll go straight down to the quarterdeck."

"No reason, sir," Masters answered.

"Phone if you want me," Murrell told him and hung up the receiver.

When he reached the stern he saw Gray stripped to bathing shorts. Oxygen cylinders were strapped to the gunner's back, and his eyes regarded his captain steadily from behind the goggled facepiece. Murrell, jealous of the man's physique, saw him set off in statuesque comparison to the oilskinned and sea-booted men who helped to adjust his gear. Gray had tied a length of light rope under his armpits, so that he could be hauled back. He walked confidently to the rail. Murrell accompanied him. "Be careful, Guns," he said. "If you can't do it, we'll find some other way." Neither man thought there was one. Gray climbed over the rail, and, taking the end of wire rope that was handed to him, he began to lower himself down the cable.

The wire rope ended in a hook that was to be put into one of the links of the cable. One party of men on deck let this rope go slowly as another party tended the lifeline. A wave lashed at Gray and swung him sideways — and another. The gunner looked up and waved cheerfully. For a moment the ship was still. Seizing the opportunity, he slipped quickly down, paused while he adjusted a valve and then, in a flurry of kicking legs, disappeared.

Murrell waited among the men on deck. Because each man in his own imagination was down there under the sea, fighting the movement of the ship and the pull and tug of the water, no one spoke. A torpedoman was holding a stop watch. Gray had asked to be pulled up after seven minutes. Both the rope and the wire had been paid out, the amount of wire judged by the length of rope. When loosed, the light rope lay on the water. As Gray moved down the chain, the rope snaked after him — a measure of his passage. After three minutes it had ceased to be drawn down. Gray had evidently got far enough, or as far as he could.

There followed four minutes of acute anxiety. While the rope had been going down, they knew that Gray was still working. When the rope stopped, there was no knowledge. When you didn't know,

Murrell thought, you either had no worry, or you worried too much and needlessly. Murrell watched the second hand of his own watch complete another circle.

Then men were stirring beside him, shifting feet that had been held long without movement. A voice laughed in too high a pitch. Gray came to the surface. His arms and legs moved slowly, clutching the cable. Leading Seaman Thomas pushed past the Captain. He had a line tied around his waist and was stripped to his pants and vest. He began to climb down to Gray's assistance. Afterwards no one was quite sure how they managed to get them both aboard.

Gray, supported by two sailors, was half dragged, half carried, to the after house. His body was dappled blue with cold, and there was a nasty gash on his shoulder. The doctor waited to tend him, but Gray turned and indicated that he wished to speak to the Captain. Someone had taken off his face mask. "It's hooked on, sir," he said, "about a fathom below the rudder. The chain *was* over the forrard upper corner — as Chiefey said."

"Well done, you," Murrell said, feeling any words to be quite inadequate.

A signalman forced his way through the crowd. Murrell took the pad. There were two signals. The first from Admiralty read, "Wireless traffic in your vicinity suggests you have been sighted by enemy aircraft." The second was from Wheeler: it said, "Am ready to take tow on port cable."

"Reply to *Antioch,*" Murrell said to the signalman. "Think we have got to the bottom of our trouble, but it will be another hour before we are ready to tow," and, "You'd better repeat that signal from Admiralty to the *Antioch* 'for information' — and the one we had last night about their having no tug to send us."

When they came to haul the hawser aboard they found that the big rope, which on the previous afternoon had been dry and soft to handle, was now cold, wet, stiff and a very great deal heavier. It stuck in the fair-lead; and as all the men not on watch struggled to drag it along the deck it refused to bend. Then, when they had finally forced it to do so, it kinked. Stronger than any boa constrictor, it took a half-turn around itself. It had to be fought continually, until, when one length was finally defeated, it could be lashed down to the rails or any other handy place to keep it quiet until they were ready to pass the tow again.

It was eleven o'clock before the *Hecate* was once more ready for the *Antioch,* and mid-day when the tanker was again hitched up. By then the visibility was so improved that they could see the real horizon.

With the breaking of the cloud layer; the seas had assumed their normal blue, and, where the wind-driven crests overbalanced, white tendrils of foam formed patches of lace. As a result of the clearing, the wind had shifted from south to north of west, and the change of tow from the starboard to the port cable of the *Antioch* suited the new conditions. With the shift had come the first pale sunshine they had seen for more than forty-eight hours; but, as the barometer had gone up, the thermometer had gone down. The wind that now blew before it the tattered remnants of the clouds was cold enough to penetrate the heaviest clothing. It set Murrell shivering as he stood at the after end of the bridge, conning the ship, and waiting for half past twelve when he was due to be relieved by the doctor.

Macmillan, arriving, asked, "How does she go?"

"Not too well," the Captain said as he took off the telephone. "That wretched length of cable hanging from the starboard bow is making her even more bitchy than usual. I'll have to tell Wheeler he must get it in somehow."

"In the meantime," Macmillan said, "your ship is happier with her tow than she was yesterday ... I refer, of course, to the men."

"I hadn't noticed it," Murrell said.

"Oh, it's there all right. Moving about the ship as I do, I have my ear pretty close to the ground — all right, I know it's a wrong metaphor, but you know what I mean. The men are much happier. Man can get used to almost anything — but it's more than that. They are becoming just a little proud of her."

"Or of themselves?" Murrell asked, and went on, "Not that it matters which."

"Not at the moment it doesn't," Macmillan said, "but it might."

Murrell felt too tired, hungry and cold to embark with the recently fed doctor on one of the discussions he so much loved. "I'm going to write out two signals to *Antioch*. Then I'm going to have my lunch," he said, "and afterwards, please God, I'll have a sleep until four."

He went into the chart house and wrote down two signals to be passed to the tow. "As soon as possible you should do your utmost to get in your starboard cable. It is adversely affecting the tow." And another: "As soon as opportunity permits you should inspect your A.A. armament and arrange to bring as much as possible into action if we are attacked. Preference should be given to Oerlikon or Bofors rather than to the four-inch gun. Report results so that I may know what help I may expect from you. Suggest one man to each Oerlikon and two men on the Bofors. Fire a few rounds from all guns for practice after 1600 tonight."

When, after eating the lunch that Kirby had brought, he flung himself on his bunk, his last thoughts before sleep were that the men might be happier, and he was glad of it, but he himself could never be happy while his ship felt so heavy.

He dreamed, and in his dream found himself, with two friends of pre-war days, running down the seemingly endless passage of a great hotel. And as they ran they played with an alarm clock as if it were a football, bouncing it on the ground and passing it from one to another. Idly, he wondered what sort of party had led to this prank. Doors were opened behind them and voices called out angrily. Bang, went the alarm clock on the floor. Bending low he caught and passed it neatly to Charles. Then it wasn't an alarm clock any longer. It was just a noise. Clunk. Clunk.

Someone knocked at his door. He struggled furiously to rid himself of the cloak of exhaustion that seemed to smother him, and fought off the blankets. "Come in," he gasped.

A signalman was at his side. "Signal from aircraft, sir." Murrell, propping his shoulders on the pillows, tried to read. But his eyes were blurred with sleep and he had difficulty in focussing the pencilled words. Then, as the import melted the mists of his brain, the writing became intensely clear. "Have attacked U-boat approximately twenty miles 270 degrees from your position. Enemy was steaming 090 degrees fast. Fear attack did nothing but annoy. He sighted me in time to dive. Have reached prudent limit of endurance and am going home now. See you tomorrow."

"Thank you, Reeves," Murrell handed the pad back. "I suppose he sent that and went."

"Yes, sir. He was going away fast. I was only just able to read the end of the message." Reeves disappeared through the door.

Murrell raised himself purposefully from his bunk. "See you tomorrow," he murmured. "I hope to God he's right!"

Wheeler and his six men had had a back-breaking morning, and Murrell's signal suggesting that they haul in the starboard cable had been received with determined but cold resolution. As seamen, they could not fault the order; as men they felt that they had had enough. They had had no time to experiment with the galley fire, and so no chance to try the recipe that had been sent over for dealing with their macaroni. The cold meat that they had eaten for their dinner had restored energy, but not warmth, to their bodies.

The seven sat on their mattresses and huddled their blankets around them for warmth. With more than twenty-four hours' stubble on all their chins they looked a far more desperate crew than in fact they were. The air was gray and stale with the smoke of seven Greek cigarettes. Wheeler thought the cold smell the worst of their discomforts. The men were complaining at the contents of the morning's signal, and he feared that this, the first chance of discussion, might well cut the slender support that carried the morale of his crew. Even so, it seemed better to let them have the short respite that would be measured by the time to smoke a cigarette than to drive them out immediately to face the heavy work of getting rid of the cable — whatever unwelcome thoughts would be aired in the meantime.

"So they can't find no tug for us?" Pengelley asked of no one in particular.

Wheeler guessed the words to have been really pointed at him. Doing his best to support authority in general, he told them:

"Tugboats lead a pretty busy life. We're not the only damaged ship that's waiting for a tow."

"As far as I'm concerned, sir, it's us what matter." Pengelley spoke defiantly. "I've had about enough of this commission."

"That goes for me too," Sibson said with truculence. "If I could get off this crate, I'd go. Here and now, I'd go. Just like that. I knows how to lie-up when the police are after me. They'd not catch me for a deserter!"

"There's experience talking!" Anders, speaking to White, chose a bad moment to taunt Sibson.

"If I weren't so flipping cold, I'd knock your bloody block off." Sibson stirred uneasily. "Come to think of it — I'm not certain that I won't." He half rose to lean across White and push his face towards Anders.

"If you can't be quiet, we'll go out to the job!" Wheeler was calling on all his authority.

Hart came to his officer's aid. "Oh, stow it, you bloody fools. Ain't we got enough on our plate without that. Supposing the bloody tug does come — who gets us off? Like as not, you'll have to stay here. And then you'd only have a tug to look after you 'stead of a destroyer. You ought to be thankful we got her with us."

"Don't we count for anything?" Trotman asked.

"Not for a damn thing, you don't. Not when there's a war on," Hart told him.

"And yet, if we was stuck down a ruddy coal mine, there'd be no end of a shindig to get us out. Queer, ain't it?" Anders said. "Feeling no one gives a damn!"

"You're a 'listed man," Hart told him. "You're expendable."

"If that Jerry aircraft did report us, the tug and escorts won't be along in time." Anders spoke sadly.

"Every roll." White was talking to himself more than to the others. "Every roll. You expects every roll to be the last."

Wheeler said, "Stop it! The staff ashore are not inhuman. We've just got to wait until they can send out the right bits and pieces to get us home, that's all." He stubbed out his cigarette. "Come on — let's get the cable in. With that lot dragging in the water, she can't be expected to tow straight." He got to his feet.

"Anyway," Pengelley said as he got up, "work will keep us warm. Ain't it flipping cold?" He followed Wheeler through the door. The others, all except Sibson, followed.

Sibson had been last to rise. He shouted after them, "What's the use of working on something that isn't going to last!" But the others had gone too far to hear him. Perhaps he would really have refused duty. But with the sudden inrush of silence after the others had gone, he could not bear to be alone. "Hi, you — wait for me," he called, and hurried after them.

Arrived on the fo'c's'le, they gazed at the task before them. The big cable rose from the cable locker and, instead of passing over the whelps of the winch, it lay on the deck. It was held by a slip stopper, fastened to a big lug that was bolted to the deck beams. The cable was so heavy that only with short lengths of rope passed through the links had they been able to move it at all. And that was yesterday when it had only had to be lifted from the cable locker. Now three hundred feet of it hung down into the sea, and it weighed more than fifty tons.

Fortunately they had found two four-fold tackles, and, arranging these so that one pulled on the fall of the 'other, they set to work. But it was desperately slow. When they had hauled the one tackle until the blocks touched each other, they had only moved the first set of blocks a foot nearer together. Then the stops had to be moved on the cable, the tackle overhauled and spread out again, and another five minutes heaving would only yield another foot won home.

Hauling the tackle was not easy on the swaying deck. They had, when they hauled, a corporate unity — but only as the tail of a dog, with its jointed bones, can be said to have unity. The first man on the rope, being nearest to the point that was a fixture, swayed less than the third, and much less than the seventh. As the *Antioch* rolled, so did the sweating, cursing line of men wag.

But they went on trying. At the end of two hours they had brought in twenty feet of cable, and they were all worn out. Then suddenly Hart began to laugh. He laughed wildly and held his sides until tears ran down his cheeks.

There is always something deeply disturbing about laughter that is out of place. Men have been shot for less — and with reason. Hart's laughter suggested madness, and there was no man there who did not feel his own brain reel. The immediate effect was to make each let go of the rope. Then, to their consternation at the laughter was added the chagrin of seeing at least a foot of the heavy cable lurch outboard once more. It was a sight that brought individual fury and a state that threatened collective mutiny.

Pengelley sat down with his back to the winch. "I've flipping well had it!" he said. "You can do what you like with that lot — an' for Christ's sake stop that cackling!" He put his hands to his ears and sank his head on his chest.

"Gone balmy," Trotman said, inspecting Hart carefully with tired eyes that were red-rimmed with salt.

Wheeler, feeling the situation slide, tried desperately to place normality in his own voice. He was drawn to approach Hart almost as if he would have hit him. and, despite all attempts, his own voice came to him high-pitched and desperate. "What's so funny, Hart?"

Hart stopped laughing as suddenly as he had begun. "Why, you silly buggers. If you don't want the ruddy thing — cut it off. There's shackles and shackles left in the locker — and none of it ours!"

The line of men sat down beside Pengelley. Wheeler dropped to the deck in front of them. None of them spoke. The hint of madness was there again, but this time it had more validity. Each was shamed before the others at his lack of common sense. And Wheeler, who knew he had to be the first to recover himself, was the most affected because he should have seen the obvious solution. It was what he was there for. "Oh, God," he thought. "Oh, Anne. You'd never do a bloody silly thing like that." But he had to say something to pull his silent men together — anything. His eyes looked down at the seams of the deck on which he crouched and his fingers played with the pitch in the seams.

"I had an aunt who went on a visit to America," he told them. "She wrote on a postcard, 'You'd never believe who I met the other day. I met cousin Mary. I can't ever tell you what a shock it was. It's too awful. I'm going to forget all about it.' "

"What had she done, sir?" Anders asked.

"That's just the point," Wheeler said. "My aunt was killed in an air crash on the way home, and so we never found out. Whatever cousin Mary had done was completely hidden. I mean, that's what we all want to do about today's foolishness."

"I expect she'd turned tart, sir," Anders said, making it obvious to Wheeler that, even if it had restarted conversation, as a parable his tale had misfired.

At last Wheeler was able to laugh naturally. "Come on then — let's cut it off." He got to his feet.

## Chapter 9

U-506 hustled over the ocean. On the bridge Lachmann, with Braun, the Officer of the Watch, and a seaman lookout clustered around the periscope standards. Up in the keen air, and close to the hissing seas, the excitement of the chase tensed every nerve. What was below an almost intolerable clatter of the diesels working at maximum power was heard in the conning tower as a steady and companionable drone; and the vibration, which was excessive in the narrow overcrowded mess decks, they felt as the expectant quivering of a mettlesome horse.

Time and again glasses would be raised to the horizon to look for the tiny upright stick that would be the first sight of their quarry, and continually one or the other would search the sky, in case an inquisitive British air patrol should interfere.

But the sky was empty. And the hard horizon below the cumulus clouds, which looked so deceptively serene, was only notched by jagged wavetops. For the moment, it was an enchanted scene. The swift boat running among hurrying waves whose backs looked deceptively smooth and gentle as they passed ahead of the high and graceful bow in continuously undulating succession.

It was Lieutenant Braun who saw it first. *"Herr Kapitän. Herr Kapitän!* There. Just beneath that cloud. Painted white and difficult to see. There now. Look. She comes out into that patch of blue." Lachmann spun around. His glasses were held halfway up to his face as he strove to see with the naked eye what his junior described, before he narrowed his field of vision by looking through the glasses — which a wise man used for identification rather than detection.

*"Ja,"* he grunted, "I have it now. Your eyesight, *Herr Leutnant,* is excellent." The intruder had been sighted sufficiently far away to permit of his diving to a safe depth before ever she had the chance to attack him.

Certainly it would be very annoying to be forced to dive. The next sixty minutes were most crucial, for during that time he had hoped to sight the masts of the tanker.

"Slow, both engines," he ordered. It was always possible that they had not yet been seen. The aircraft was five miles north of him, and steering west. He had her in silhouette against the hard northern sky, but she would be looking into the sun at a vast expanse of wave-flecked water. At that distance the airmen might well overlook the very small blob that the U-boat would be.

Breathlessly the Germans watched. Apparently unconcerned, the aircraft moved sedately across the sky, appearing as a white dot against the blue, and becoming almost invisible when she crossed the masses of gray-white cloud.

"The 'Ube' has reduced speed — I'm afraid she's spotted us," Flight-Lieutenant Leathers, the second pilot of the Sunderland, spoke over his shoulder to the aircraft's captain.

"In this visibility, Tony, she could hardly help it."

"Will you attack at once?" Leathers asked.

While the aircraft flew on, the Captain thought. Then the gyro began to tick slowly as Squadron Leader Jackson gave his craft slight — very slight — left rudder. "I think not," he answered, speaking carefully. "As I see it, time is the essence of this contract. That bird is obviously chasing those two poor suckers. Someone, probably a German recce plane, has spotted our friends; or perhaps another Ube. But that particular sardine tin is after them for a certainty. The longer we can delay him, the less chance he has to find them. I reckon we'll play with him until we've used up all the time we've juice for. Then we'll run in and make him dive. When he can see us so plainly, we haven't an earthly chance of getting in a good attack. But, by the time he's recovered from the shock, it'll be dam' nigh dark — and he'll loathe our guts. Did anybody, by any chance, say something about coffee?"

*"Herr Kapitän.* He is turning. He is the same distance away. That I am sure. But his bearing has altered almost ninety degrees since we first saw him," Braun said.

"He is turning very slowly to the southward," Lachmann answered. "I do not think, *Herr Leutnant,* that he has seen us."

"The sun is the devil. I can not see him. When I have the dark filter down, I can see nothing; but without a filter my eyes are blinded." Lachmann spoke savagely.

"He is steering south, *Herr Kapitän."*

"I still do not think he has seen us. Let us wait."

"I am tired of waiting — and yet to increase speed is to be seen. He has already wasted twenty minutes of our time. What is he doing now?" Lachmann asked.

"It appears that he flies round and round in small circles, *Herr Kapitän."* Braun's voice betrayed his bewilderment.

"So I see," Lachmann snapped. "God in heaven! Why should I be cursed with this acrobatic fool at this hour of the day." Exasperated, the Germans watched without speaking as first one wing of their persecutor was seen to tilt, and then the other. The plane, after making a tight turn to port, followed it with one to starboard. Then, as if pleased with its performance, it made a figure eight the other way around. Then it came down slowly, almost to sea level, and rose again.

Lachmann, watching it, dropped his binoculars and beat his hands fiercely against the rail of the cockpit. "This is too much," he exploded.

Neither of his companions answered him. The sailor certainly dared not do so. The officer, realizing his captain's dilemma, could not think of any way in which he could show the sympathy he felt: not that he had a great deal of that, for in common with all the rest of the crew he wished that their previous captain had not been taken away from them. Then no mistake would have been made over the tanker.

73

The plane was lower now, circling down again. *Herr Kapitän, Herr Kapitän,* I think he is closing us!" Braun said.

"But if he could not see us from high up, how can he see us from low down?" Lachmann wanted to know.

"I think myself, *Herr Kapitän,* that he has seen us all the time. He just plays with us."

"Nonsense, *Herr Leutnant.* It is not possible."

"He is coming in, *Herr Kapitän.* Will you dive, or shall I man the gun?"

"Dive, damn you, dive." Lachmann's finger felt for the button that would sound the klaxon.

As U-506 sank purposefully into the depths, the Sunderland, its big propellers beating their fastest, came down-sun with the wind on its port quarter. But she had not the speed, nor had she the quick-sinking depth charges that a year later she would have carried.

If Lachmann's U-boat received no more than a fright and a severe shaking, she had been robbed of a vital hour of daylight.

## Chapter 10

When Murrell reached the bridge it was illuminated by the setting sun. The rays, almost parallel with the winter sea, had no heat. The men gathered there appeared in a light that came from one side, and, like actors on a stage where there are only footlights, their faces had an unreal and paper-thin quality. By contrast, the eyes that followed the Captain as he moved thoughtfully past the compass platform to the chart house all held the same and very real query, "What is he going to do about it?" They all knew of the signal. It had been passed by light from the aircraft, and the signalman had called out each word as it had been received.

Murrell thought that by this time there would be few in the ship who did not know. The tendrils of the grapevine led everywhere except to the engine and boiler rooms. In these spaces the men did not immediately learn the "buzzes" that filtered down from the bridge. They had to wait until the watch was relieved or some out-of-the-ordinary occurrence gave them the chance to meet the better-informed men on deck. But almost everyone now would be expecting him to pull out of the hat some rabbit that would allay their personal fears. And as he felt inside it, the hat seemed to be remarkably empty.

"Port twenty. Slow port." He heard Graves' voice repeat the doctor's order. For the moment he had quite forgotten the *Antioch*. Ever since the tow started, his first action on coming on deck had been to look to see how the tow was behaving. Now, with the appearance of the enemy, the *Antioch* had taken second place. Realizing this, he went out onto the side of the bridge to look at the merchant ship, not because he really wanted to see her, but because it gave him more time to search inside the hat.

"How's she go?" he asked, coming up behind the doctor.

"Much as usual, sir," Macmillan spoke over his shoulder. Then, "Starboard five. Half ahead together."

Murrell went back to the chart house. There was something in the hat after all; a nebulous germ that grew to coherent thought, and then blossomed into a definite idea. "Mr. Graves. Has Gray recovered from his bathing party yet .

"He ate a damn good lunch, sir, and got his head down this afternoon," Graves told him.

"Pass the word for him to come to the bridge," Murrell said.

With the first words from their captain, the tension among the men showed signs of being relaxed. Action was going to be taken. They were not so much interested in what was to be done as that something — anything — should be attempted. They did not expect the impossible; and if a torpedo should rip its way into the delicate hull of their ship they would not, as long as some effort had been made to counter the wiles of the enemy, blame their captain.

However inadequate he might feel, Murrell knew he had to keep up his counterfeit of omnipotence. He went slowly into the chart house as though to study the chart. In reality his mind was busy with the apparently absurd idea that had come to him.

To continue on this course was to invite disaster. The U-boat would surface again within an hour of the aircraft's departure and be hot on his trail once more. At the very slow speed of the tow, an alteration of course would be useless unless it was a very large one — almost ninety degrees. But the tow would probably behave better beam-on to the sea, and they might be able to go a little faster. Which way to turn? Or, more important, which way would the enemy expect him to turn? If the captain of the Sunderland had been right in his deduction that the U-boat was specifically chasing them, it implied that the Germans *did* know his position. The Admiralty had been right. He had obviously been sighted either by a patrolling German aircraft or, a worse thought, by another U-boat. The daily report in which the Admiralty assessed the position of the U-boats gave only one as being in their area. For the moment the North Atlantic was fairly free. The German U-boat Command, worried by the way the escorts had been detecting their boats at night, had sent the bulk of their forces to annoy the Americans in the Caribbean.

With the chart of Western Approaches to the British Isles before him, Murrell studied the position. The top right-hand corner of the chart showed the Hebrides, and at the bottom right-hand corner the headland of Ushant jutted out into the Atlantic. Ushant, the German-occupied French headland, attracted his attention; for it was odds-on that when the captain of the U-boat came to decide his own tactics, he would be using an almost exactly similar chart — and Ushant would be "home" to him.

Surely the German would expect him to turn to the northward and away from the occupied territory? He thought so. He had to choose one way or the other. He noted, however, that to turn to the south would make no difference to their own air cover. For, though he would be going slightly nearer to Ushant, he would be no further away from the Irish coast. He must keep the Commander-in-Chief advised of the position, and, as the enemy must have a good idea of his present whereabouts, that signal should be made before he turned.

He had thought thus far when a shadow darkened the doorway of the chart house. "You wanted me, sir?" It was Gray's voice — full of confidence.

"Yes, indeed." Murrell smiled. He was pleased to see him, and the Commissioned Gunner's own smile brought a reflection to the lips of those to whom he spoke. "Have you recovered from your swimming party? Incidentally, I hope that earns you something that we can have a party to celebrate. It ought to do so; but I expect it will depend, like so many things, on our success with our problem child. If we get her in, we'll be clapped on the back. If we don't we'll get our bottoms spanked."

"Quite recovered, sir, and thank you," Gray said.

"You've heard about the U-boat?" Murrell asked.

Gray nodded, "Yes, sir."

"I want to arrange a little deception. Something to draw the enemy away from us and give our Germanic friends something to chase."

"You mean a false trail, sir?" Gray asked.

"Yes, a sort of conjuring trick. Something which will look like a ship, but isn't." Murrell turned to see the mystified look on the weather-beaten face, which, in the confined space of the chart house, was pressed close to his own. He laughed. "A light would do it, you know, Guns — just a little light. With no moon and the stars veiled, the night will be as black as the Earl of Hell's riding boots. You'd not see an unlighted ship more than a quarter of a mile away — but the Germans would see a light when they're a good six miles off it. I hope they'll chase it, and I hope they'll waste time stalking it. Something like a Carley Float with a lamp on it — as high up as we can get it. I had thought of a dan buoy, but it would wave about too much. If we were to rig a bearing-out spar as a mast on a Carley Float, and put a dan-buoy light on top of the spar, it would be about eighteen feet above the water — the height of the portholes in the tanker's stern. I intend to make a ninety-degree alteration of course to starboard as soon as, or just before, we slip the contraption, so you can arrange to put it into the water with the port torpedo davit. It won't weigh very much. Do you get the idea?"

"Yes, sir. Indeed I do!"

Murrell, seeing the light in Gray's eyes, decided that he had been right to choose him for the preparation of the machine. "Right. Cut along and get the work started. I want it ready in an hour. It will be dark by then. I've a signal to make to the tow and one to Western Approaches. Then I'll be down to see how you are getting on."

When Gray had left, Murrell called for the Yeoman. He wondered what message to send to the *Antioch*. He wondered if he should tell them of the threat? He fancied that no good ever came of withholding vital information from the men, except those secret matters where talk ashore might endanger themselves or their companions. Once a ship was at sea, the more they knew of the immediate problems, the more use they would be. The more they understood, the less the danger from disinterested tiredness, and, while improving their own chances of survival, it made the ship a more formidable foe for the enemy to meet. He took the pad that the Yeoman gave him.

*"Hecate* to *Antioch.* Aircraft has reported U-boat presumably chasing us twenty miles astern. Aircraft forced U-boat to dive. Presume it will not surface until dark. In order to reduce chance of interception intend to alter course ninety degrees to starboard at 1700. At the same time launching raft carrying dan-buoy light to

decoy enemy. If enemy is detected during night I intend to slip tow and attack. Goodnight, and keep smiling."

Murrell tore off the signal and handed it to the Yeoman. "Get that off while I write a message to the Commander-in-Chief," he said.

The next signal was more difficult. *"Hecate* to C-in-C, Western Approaches. In view of aircraft's report of U-boat approaching from westward, intend to alter course at 1700 to the southward during night, resuming my course for Bloody Foreland at daybreak tomorrow. My position at 1700 today will be 54° 18' N. 19° 45' W. Am making four knots and hope to maintain this unless weather deteriorates. Request tomorrow's aircraft be informed."

The first signal was being passed by signalman Reeves. Murrell could hear the clickety-clack of the lamp. The Yeoman was waiting for the second signal. The expression on his face reminded Murrell of a bird that hovers around a fountain. The simile, once thought of, made him smile, and he went out onto the open bridge revitalized. "Here you are, Yeoman. Have it coded up and sent as soon as ready." The Captain crossed to join the doctor. The watch was changing, and the bridge held twice its normal complement of men. There was chatter too, as those who had been on watch passed on the news to their reliefs. It was four o'clock.

"Sorry, Doc, but I'll have to ask you to hang on for another hour. I'm going to launch a decoy at five, and turn to the southward during the night. Are you all right?"

"I wondered what it was that 'Guns' was making down there," Macmillan said. "Can do." Then he bent his head to the mouthpiece. "Starboard twenty. Slow starboard."

So the interminable tow went on, with the voice of the conning officer as important a link as any in the cable that connected the two ships.

Down below on the long deck, which was only eight feet clear of the waves, the sea had an aspect quite different from the one it showed to those who lived mainly on the bridge. Murrell was always surprised by the change. From forty feet above the surface, a wave would appear as one of a series; but from the lower level each had an entity of its own, had its own character, and bore its own threat. By coming down from the bridge he had changed his view from that of an officer who stood on a saluting basis to that of a man marching in the ranks.

Gray had already made a start. The bearing-out spar, its heel suitably lashed, and with the small electric light secured to its head, was being fitted with stays to keep it upright. For some minutes the Captain watched the work. Then his eye was caught by the masts of the lost whaler, which, in their gray canvas bags, were secured by metal straps under the supports of the midship Oerlikon guns.

"How would it be to give it a sail?" Murrell suggested to Gray. "We could set up the whaler's jib on that stay you've just fitted; then the raft would sail downwind and really give the light the appearance of moving."

"Don't see why not, sir. Those inflatable rubber dinghies that the airmen use — they blow downwind fast enough. Remember the one we tried to get aboard a month since? Lor' love you, it was like trying to get a lump of quicksilver alongside."

The bag was taken down, the sail taken out and bent on. Once set, it gave promise of pulling so well that it had to be rolled up and lashed until the craft was ready for launching.

"Pity we haven't got a prisoner, sir," Leading Seaman Thomas said as he worked. "We could put him aboard and let him sail home — with the chance of being picked up again by 'is pals."

The suggestion was valueless in itself, but it served to raise a laugh, and mirth made the job go more easily. It made Murrell think out one move more. "You know, Gray, there is something in Thomas' remark. Not that I'd put a prisoner aboard — even if we had one. But I don't see why we shouldn't help it to sail itself. We might give it a tail — something like a kite."

"A couple of jerry cans lashed to the end of two fathom of warp?" Gray suggested.

"Make it six fathom, and fill the cans three-quarters full of water so they'll just float. Then I reckon we'd have the job properly weighed off."

The Captain watched the final preparations, checked over the drill to be adopted in launching the raft, and climbed back to the bridge. "Ready, Doc. I'll take her — and thank you for the extra time."

As he strapped the harness on his chest, he wished that he had had more time to think. The doctor had relieved him at half past twelve and it was nearly five o'clock. But during that time he had been able to snatch only one and a half hours' sleep, and he had so far never succeeded in having more than two hours consecutively since the towing had started. "Watch and watch" might sound all right with its promise of four hours on and four hours off. But it never gave four hours of sleep. His ship had to be run, his body had to be washed and fed, the enemy was an intermittent interference, and the weather a perpetual one.

He glanced at his watch. He could just make out the figures in the gathering dusk. Five o'clock, 1700 hours. The lanyard of the siren hung near his hand. He pulled it sharply. He had better, he thought, indicate to the tow that he was turning, even though they could not steer their own ship. It gave a pleasing normality to proceedings that were far from normal, and in the observance of routine at that moment lay the suggestion of safety through the night.

When he had made the sound signal, he gave the order for the turn. "Starboard twenty. Half ahead both engines."

Watching the towing hawser as the *Hecate* came out to starboard of her tow, he could see the bulky shape begin to follow her around. The cable was drawn across the *Antioch's* bow, and he could no longer see the hawse pipe from which it led. The *Hecate's* screws tore purposefully into the waves. The motion which had been a succession of forward swoops snubbed by the tow became one in which a sharp roll was the main feature. The men, clustered around the decoy, struggled backwards and forwards as the ship lurched. Murrell could see that the davit, normally used for hoisting torpedoes aboard the ship, had now been turned outboard. From its head, the raft, carrying its light and its sail, hung over the side. The little light burned brightly on top of its spar. In the radiance it cast, he could see Gray directing the launch. Then Gray's face was turned towards the bridge. Murrell motioned downward with his hand. With a splash, the raft hit the water and at once began to drift astern. The

81

sail, a dark smudge against the gray water, filled, and the machine sailed off steadily downwind.

The men had watched the launching with interest. Just beneath Murrell's feet the bridge messenger was talking to a coder. "Chucking away life rafts. There goes ten men's flipping lives!"

It was a criticism that Murrell had expected and discounted. The sort of calculated chance that had to be taken. "You're looking at it in quite the wrong way, Talbot," Murrell said, enjoying the consternation that he knew his interruption would cause. "You want to think that it may be saving the lives of two hundred. And," he continued, bending down to confirm what he thought he was almost sure to find, "if you'd wear your inflatable life jacket, as the Admiralty direct and my Standing Orders demand, you'd be in less danger of losing your own silly life." Satisfied, Murrell returned to his Olympian detachment. Jove had spoken. He had no doubt that within an hour the story would be told all over the ship. The encounter had not been unfortunate.

He raised his glasses. The tow was around now. "Port. twenty." Astern of the rolling *Hecate* the tanker wallowed. And already far distant on the port quarter was the little light of the decoy. At that distance it had a most satisfying resemblance to the light that might be supposed to show from the unshut porthole of a merchantman. Borne downwind and down-sea, it had just the right rise and fall. It should, Murrell thought, be good for at least two hours of wasted German effort.

## Chapter 11

Wheeler, who had been prepared to blame himself for his lack of thought over the cable, found that his men were in no mood to reproach him for their unnecessary labour. All felt equally guilty of the same lack of foresight. Only Hart had benefited. In their relief, it had been easy for his companions to forgive him his laughter, and, even if belated, his simple sagacity had won him a stature among the crew beyond that of his age. Under Wheeler he had become the real leader of the men.

A few minutes' work with a hacksaw, followed by a sharp blow with a sledge hammer, severed a link of the chain; and what had been a detriment to the tow, of which they had been unable to rid themselves, was now a pile of cable on the sea bed. For Wheeler it was a lesson learned. He now saw that to become so engrossed in manual labour was to lose the attribute of standing back and observing the job as a whole. In struggling with the trees, he had missed seeing the wood. There *was* something in the proverbs, and the Navy's dictum that officers should never work with the men had been proved to have reason behind it.

White had been able to read most of the signal made by the Sunderland aircraft, and so the *Hecate's* signal occasioned no surprise: only gratification that steps were being taken to confound the enemy. The Antiochs watched the launching of the decoy with interest, all except Hart and Sibson, who had taken themselves off to investigate the stove. Their endeavours were now rumoured to be on the point of achieving success, and they were already promising the others a hot meal by eight o'clock that night. Without electricity to drive the fan, it was impossible to light the oil fire, but when the burner had been removed, they found that the firebox was large enough to burn wood. Wheeler agreed that during daylight hours one man alone could keep watch with White. This would allow the others to chop up wood and tend the fire.

Wheeler had had time to inspect the armament. There were four Oerlikon guns, one on each wing of the bridge and one each side of the after superstructure on either side of the funnel. Behind the funnel, on the upper deck, there was a Bofors, and a four-inch gun on the boat deck. More fortunate still, the weapons were in tolerably good condition. With one man to each Oerlikon and two on the Bofors they could fight five guns, with Wheeler as spare man wherever he should be most wanted. Without electricity for the bells or compressed air for the siren, they had no method of sounding a general alarm until Pengelley discovered an old-fashioned hand foghorn in the fo'c'sle. Taken to the bridge, this answered the purpose.

Tired out, the Antiochs settled down for their second night, but with the satisfaction that the unknown and unfriendly habitation of the previous night had, with the provision of hot food, now become a ship — their ship.


"Fourteen meters, *Herr Kapitän.*" Braun's incisive voice announced the return of U-506 — if not to the surface, at least to a depth where she could use her periscope.

With the subdued hiss of high-pressure air, the big periscope rose from its well. Lachmann grasped the handles as it came within reach, and, placing his forehead against the thick rubber pad, pressed his eyes to the eye-cups. On one handle of the periscope a lever worked the prism that enabled the sky to be searched as soon as the instrument was clear of the water.

"It is dark. Too dark to see if that confounded aircraft is still about — but not dark enough for us to surface." Lachmann's speech, more than usually clipped, betrayed his impatience. No one in the control room ventured a reply, nor was any expected. The electric motors hummed steadily, driving the boat east at four knots. The periscope hissed softly to itself as it sank down into the well again. Lachmann mopped his face and neck with a scarlet handkerchief.

"Had it not been for that aircraft we should have been thirty miles nearer the target. We should have sighted it in daylight and worked into position to attack. Had luck been with us, we would in a few minutes from now have accomplished our mission." The *Kapitän* fidgeted, and glanced from face to face of those who stood or sat at their diving stations around him. "It will take us two hours at least to make up what we have lost. If we surface at half past five, we should be very close to them by seven thirty. The moon is new, and sets very early tonight, but with luck we may find some glow from the northern lights."

There was silence in the control room — and very little movement. The minutes ticked by. For the twentieth time Lachmann consulted his watch. "Surface," he ordered. The hum of the motors increased. The whistle and rattle of the high-pressure air that blew the water from the ballast tanks was plainly heard. The bow of the boat canted upwards. As she was caught by the movement of the surface waves she began to pitch steadily. Lachmann was halfway up the ladder. His hands gripped the wheel that operated the conning tower hatch. Then his feet were going up the ladder. Cold night air flowed invigoratingly into the boat. The hum of the electric motors was replaced by the rising clatter of the diesels as speed was increased once more to fifteen knots.

U-506 had surfaced, and was off in pursuit.


At eight o'clock that night the doctor came to relieve Murrell. "How is she behaving now?" he asked.

"Different kettle of fish altogether. On this course I've only had to give about half the helm orders. With the wind on the port beam I'm just nicely sheltered here — and the heat of the forward funnel takes the bite out of the wind. Really, it's quite pleasant!"

"Ever tried writing advertisements for health resorts? You make this patch of deck sound like a Lido."

"Well, it's a lot better than the other course, and that's a fact. See you at midnight."

Murrell hurried below because, before he snatched at sleep, he had a problem to consider. He had known that it had to be faced, but so far there had been too much to do, and he had relegated it to the back of his mind. The tow had presented so many difficulties that this had seemed better left until he must meet it. If, to attack the enemy, he had to slip the tow, how was he to pick it up again?

He took a pencil and pad from his desk and drew the *Antioch's* bow at one side. From this, at an angle reaching down to the waterline and below, he drew in a chain of circles which was the tanker's cable, two hundred and seventy feet long. Then there was the swivel they had fitted that morning, some ten feet in length; and lastly, three hundred feet of their own hawser. He drew this hawser in a straight line running to the stern of his own ship, which just showed on the opposite side of the paper. Where this hawser led over his own stern there was thirty feet of heavy chain.

He had only the one towing hawser, and if he had to disconnect the hawser at his end how could he connect up again? There was no winch in the stern of a destroyer, and even had there been one it would have been unlikely to be able to handle a sixty-ton haul.

Somehow or other that cable had to be buoyed — and buoyed with something that would float well clear of the tanker. The merchantman would be beam-on and drifting down-sea. Six hundred feet of three-inch manila on the *Hecate's* end of the hawser, buoyed with something that had little windage but yet would keep it afloat? It would only have to support the weight of the hawser, negligible in water, and ten hundredweight of cable. A Carley Float, or, better still, two Carley Floats lashed one on top of the other; and let the last twenty fathom of the manila go from the Carley Floats to a dan buoy. Then that in its turn, having more grip on the water, would lie upwind of the floats, and the line between the two could readily be secured with a grapnel thrown from his ship.

Hastily he drew the sketch of what he wanted. But who was to do it? Thompson had had the Dog Watch and must be on deck at four in the morning. Masters was on watch now, and Graves had to be up for the Middle. It looked like another job for Gray. While he waited for the gunner to answer his summons, he thought that undoubtedly Talbot and his like would be upset by the sight of two more life rafts being used, but again it was a calculated risk calmly taken. With one whaler lost, one raft used for the decoy, and two more about to be used to buoy the hawser, their life-saving equipment was down to three rafts — only enough to support thirty men out of the two hundred aboard. But a warship could never carry enough for all her people. The rafts were the only things that would do the work he wanted of them. He would have to risk the effect on morale. He would use them.

But even when he had given Gray these further instructions, Murrell was unable to sleep until he knew for certain that, should the radar detect an echo that would send the *Hecate* off to investigate, he would be able to recover the tow he had slipped. It was ten o'clock before Gray's knock announced the job completed.


Lachmann was eating his supper in the tiny wardroom when the call reached him. In a series of bounds, during which he managed, somehow or other, to get his arms into the sleeves of his leather jacket, he stumbled into the control room, and in a moment his heavy-booted feet beat the ironrunged ladder as he disappeared from view. Braun and a seaman clung to the conning-tower coaming with their elbows. Their arched backs and hands raised to their eyes showed that both peered through glasses.

"Where is it?" Lachmann asked.

"Fine on the port bow!" Braun told him. "Sometimes when she yaws it is right ahead."

"How far away?"

"It is difficult to say, *Herr Kapitän.* As much as five miles perhaps. It is a very small light."

"Doubtless some fool Englishman has left a scuttle open. I can't see anything. Ah — I have it. So! You are right. It is a light."

Braun wondered if his *Kapitän* really thought that he would report a rising star as a light? That could happen to anyone under certain conditions; but not tonight, not with the heavy bank of cumulus clouds packed tight around the horizon.

"The destroyer must have left — otherwise she would certainly have seen that light," Lachmann remarked.

"Or she may be zigzagging ahead," Braun suggested, and at once was made to wish that he had kept silence.

"The destroyer may be a fool — but hardly so silly as to stay ahead of a ship travelling downwind as slowly as this one must be. She would, *Herr Leutnant,* patrol round and round her."

But, although he knew that he had laid himself wide open to the jibe, Lachmann's words made Braun writhe.

Sweeping down towards it at fifteen knots, they could see the light more plainly every minute. It was obviously some height above the sea, and it rose and fell steadily. "I will take her," Lachmann said. "I will go to action stations now, and reduce speed to eight knots."

"You will require the attack-table, *Herr Kapitän?* "

"If, as I think, she is stopped, she will be lying beam-on to the sea. I will spread two torpedoes on each side of the light. For the angling, yes — we will use the attack-table."

*"Jawohl, Herr Kapitän. "*

As Braun hurried down the hatch to the control room, the action alarms filled the ship with raucous sound. The bridge had rung down for slow speed, and the hydrophone operator had been asked if he could hear propeller noises. But, even with the diesels running slowly, the noise of the submarine's own propellers had been so great that the hydro-phone operator could not be sure. The engines were stopped while another listening watch was made. The U-boat slid silently and with elegance through the sea. There was absolute silence in the delicate ears of the hydrophones. Braun reported the result into the voice pipe that led to the conning tower. "Absolutely nothing, *Herr Kapitän.* Nothing."

"Very well. It is as I thought. The tanker is disabled, and the destroyer gone home. Probably they will send a tug tomorrow, or another escort. We must see they will make their journey for nothing." Then the voice pipe spoke again. "Slow ahead both engines. Prepare tubes one to four. Give the target a range of one mile and a length of four hundred feet. Bearing, right ahead; torpedo speed, forty knots; depth, fifteen feet."

Gessner, at the attack-table, set the range, bearing and distance on the machine; then threw over the switch that connected it to the angling mechanism of the torpedoes. When he moved the "length of enemy" bar to four hundred feet, the delicate mechanism of the torpedoes would be adjusted so that, when fired, they would spread out along the length of the target. "Attack-table lined up, *Herr Kapitän,*" Gessner reported.

"Tubes one to four ready, *Herr Kapitän,*" Braun reported when, each in its turn, the "ready-to-fire" lights had glowed alight.

"Steer oh-eight-five." Lachmann's voice drifted down to the quartermaster. "And steer small."

In the silence of tense atmosphere in the control room, the quartermaster could be heard muttering to himself. At slow speed it was no easy work to keep the narrow hull steady before the following sea.

"Fire!" Lachmann's voice sounded.

The boat lurched, once: "Torpedo running," the hydro-phone operator reported. Again: "Torpedo running." A third time: "Torpedo running." The last time: "Torpedo running."

"Tubes one to four fired correctly," Braun reported to Lachmann.

They waited. A minute of anxiety, while rapid calculations were made; another minute of unbelief; a third of incredulity. Surely all four torpedoes could not have missed?

Lachmann's voice came down the voice pipe — highpitched and strained. "Braun."

*"Herr Kapitän?"*

"Check all ranges and bearings on the table and then report to me here. Let no one touch the settings until I have seen them."

Braun climbed the ladder. "Well?" Lachmann asked.

"Everything is correctly set, *Herr Kapitän.*"

Lachmann turned to look forward. The light was plainly visible now.

Braun looked at it intently. There was, to his mind, something just a little wrong with it. If he could have brought himself to use such a description, he would have said to Lachmann that it looked too insubstantial. *"Herr Kapitän."* He spoke diffidently. "I think there is something odd about that light."

"What on earth do you mean?"

"Can we not close it carefully?" Braun asked.

"We are doing that, *Herr Leutnant.*"

With glasses raised the two officers studied the light.

"It is no ship," Braun remarked.

"Then what the devil is it? It can't be fishing gear — not out here. It *must* be a ship!" Lachmann sounded distraught.

"It's a decoy," Braun said.

"Nonsense," Lachmann snapped.

"It is — I can see it now. It's a tall slender pole with a light on top."

"You imagine things. I can see nothing." The *Kapitän* now sounded less certain. In reality he was shivering so much with chagrin, annoyance and mystification that he could hardly hold the binoculars to his eyes. Then at last he saw it. "Good God," he murmured, clutching the rail of the conning tower. Four torpedoes. Four of the Reich's most expensive torpedoes. Twenty thousand Reichsmarks apiece. Eighty thousand thrown away on some tomfoolery that a crazy enemy had set in the sea!

"It's got a sail on it," Braun said.

Hope leaped again in Lachmann's heart. "Survivors! Perhaps the tanker *has* sunk! I'm going alongside. Here — take my torch and go along the casing." Lachmann handed Braun the torch and watched him disappear past the antiaircraft gun to climb down to the casing.

The U-boat was overhauling the raft. All her men had learned of the fresh development, and excitement replaced mystification. Survivors — shortly they'd be prisoners. Braun, holding on to the jumping stay in the bows of the U-boat, crouched ready to shine his torch. The raft was now plainly visible by its own light, only a few feet from the U-boat's inquiring bow.

Then suddenly Braun, who had caught sight of the rope leading from the stern of the raft and the jerry cans it towed, was running aft. His boots clattered and stumbled on the deck. "It's an infernal machine — infernal machine!" he roared. "It's towing a mine!"

Lachmann heard him. "Full astern together," he ordered. It was an order that caught the engine room unawares. To go astern, diesel engines must be stopped and restarted in the opposite direction. While the men in the engine room sweated to obey the order, U-506 ran on. Her bow cut into the raft. Lachmann flung up his arm to protect his face from an explosion that did not come. The diesels, tearing the water to frenzy in their efforts to stop the boat, began to run astern. As the propellers revolved at full speed in the opposite direction, the U-boat's stern was sucked down. A wave creamed over it, and, running along her, submerged Braun as he clung, gasping, to the rail of the antiaircraft gun. The wave broke into the conning tower, soaked Lachmann to the skin; and a lot of water went down the hatch to wet the men in the control room.

When the wave had passed, Braun joined Lachmann. "What now?" he gasped, as he wiped the water from his face.

"Reload. We must dive to eighty meters, where it is quiet, and reload the four forward tubes. Then we shall search for the swine, and, God in heaven! When I find him..."


It was midnight before reloading had been completed and U-506 had once more been brought to the surface. Waiting in the control room before they came up, Lachmann had been studying the chart. "If they set off that damn-fool toy, they must have altered course," the *Kapitän* said. "And they are sure to have altered to the northward. They would never have chosen a course that would take them nearer our own coast. Therefore we shall search along this line and along that — and then this."

"You do not think, *Herr Kapitän ...*" Braun spoke with diffidence. It was obvious he had something to suggest.

"Yes, I do think. That is why we will do as I say." Lachmann's still-angry eyes turned on his junior.

Braun said nothing. He had been going to suggest the possibility that the British would have thought just that, and then have turned to the south.

Murrell, Gray and the Hecates could hardly have expected more for their money.

## Chapter 12

The following dawn was high and clear, with only a few cumulus clouds in the sky. During the night the clouds had lost their hurried, wind-blown look, and now sailed tranquilly before the wind on flat bases. But the surface wind was just as strong. At half past seven Murrell altered the course of his little party to the eastward again. At eight o'clock the doctor came up.

"She was much better behaved before," Murrell told him. "The change to a downwind course has let the devil into her again. She's trying to wander all over the ocean. Port fifteen: stop port. You've got to watch her the whole time."

"At least we'll be four miles nearer home for each hour's work," Macmillan said, pausing to polish his pipe down the side of his nose.

"It's a point," Murrell agreed. Then picking on the word "home," he said, "I've hardly dared to think about the place. Odd that, because whenever before I've had to pull myself right out to do a thing, I've always spent a lot of time thinking about it. Starboard five: half ahead together. This time, I've either been too busy, or, because the chance of getting there intact seems less, my mind has shied away from it. You ready to take over?"

Macmillan said, "Yes. I'll take her. I think the point you make is that usually the outcome has rested a great deal on your own personal prowess. This time there's so much chance about it that the individual is rather swamped."

Murrell unbuckled the chest pad and telephone. "Do you really believe the individual can be swamped?"

"Of course not!" Macmillan took the instruments. "Otherwise I wouldn't waste my life trying to mend them — I'd be off round the world alone. Mark you, I think the Eastern mind can be swamped — and maybe the African, I don't know. That's why the Oriental will lie down and die on you, or climb into an airplane and become a suicide bomber. The European mind is different." Macmillan paused to adjust the straps of the telephone pad.

Murrell said, "How about the Slav?"

"They are half and half. Not half the population one sort and half the other — but all mixed up in the same person. So with them you never know where the hell you are!"

Murrell said, "If you don't keep an eye on the *Antioch,* she's going to take you to Iceland instead of Ireland!"

The doctor took a quick glance astern. "Starboard twenty; stop starboard." He gave the order and grinned at Murrell. "That's what comes of starting discussions at this hour of the morning! I'll not forget there's an R in this month."

"Keep remembering it's February," Murrell said, and, "Good luck."

The Captain, moving away, felt better for the mental exercise that his short talk with the doctor had provided. It was even possible, he thought, that Macmillan had purposely manufactured a discussion to create the illusion of normality. For a few fleeting moments he had quite forgotten the existence of the *Antioch* and been carried outside his circle of worry. But now he was inside again. Last night he had deceived and evaded the U-boat that was looking for him. He was sure that this morning a number of very angry *Herrenvolk* would be gunning for him — and the excellent visibility would give them every chance to find their target.

A signalman, he saw and heard, was trying to pass a signal to the *Antioch,* but White was proving unusually obtuse in receiving it. "What is it, Reeves? Hasn't White got the sleep out of his eyes yet?" Murrell asked.

"Doesn't seem able to understand it, sir."

"What is it?" Murrell looked over the man's shoulder at the writing on the pad.

"Here, sir. *'Au gratin.'* Can't say I understand it myself." Reeves's finger pointed out the words.

"Try 'with cheese,' " the Captain said and passed on to the compass platform.

The lamp clicked busily as White took in the more-familiar words.

"Aircraft red five-oh." The port lookout's voice reached the Captain. "Low down. Just under that cloud," the report was amplified.

There was no mistaking the long sharklike silhouette. "Focke-Wulf reconnaissance plane," Murrell said. "We're spotted. Duty watch stand by guns. I won't go to action stations because in this visibility I don't think he'll attack. Yeoman, make to *Antioch* ... no. On second thought, don't interrupt the macaroni signal. You can make it by flag. Enemy aircraft bearing oh-five-oh."

"Radar reports range sixteen thousand, sir," Thompson informed him.

"Out of range," Murrell said. "He'll just fly round and annoy us. I know his kind. I only hope he doesn't shoot down our Sunderland. That would be a pity!"

With interest, the men on the heaving bridge watched the slim pencil that slid so smoothly under the flat base of the cloud. Never deviating from its course, it winged on southward on its way to Bordeaux, and Murrell knew that his present position would be reported to the U-boat.

The German had only just been lost to sight when another aircraft was sighted. It was coming straight toward them out of the east. The heavy body beneath the straight wing confirmed it was their Sunderland. As it came toward them a signal lamp started to blink from its white-painted side.

"Good morning. I am pleased to see you," it announced.

"Reply: Not half as pleased as I am,' " the Captain said.

"Have you .any orders?" the aircraft asked.

The signal had already been written out and given to the Yeoman. He commenced the reply at once. "Anticipate our friend of last night will try to attack. Please patrol round us, radius four miles. Look out for periscope."

Now that any underwater attacker would have to face the vigilance of the big flying boat, Murrell felt much happier. With this sea running, an enemy would need to show a lot of his periscope to carry out a submerged attack, and in the clear blue water his hull would almost certainly be seen, a dark shadow under the blue of the sea. Murrell tried to put himself in the place of the German captain.

But after some thought he decided that it was profitless to do so, if only because he did not know the character of the man that he had to face. A really skilful and determined captain could attack him at any time, day or night. But Prien was dead, and Kretschmer a prisoner-of-war. There were not many men of that supreme calibre. The average U-boat commander was a night bird by disposition and by training. Murrell fancied that the coming night, the third of the tow, would introduce him to the U-boat.

The Navigator climbed the ladder to the bridge. "Did you get your morning stars?" the Captain asked.

"Yes, sir. Two hundred and fifty miles to Bloody Foreland." Masters answered the unspoken question.

"We're getting on. I'll earn my Tug-master's Certificate yet. Any news of that anticyclone?"

"It's intensifying, sir, and stretches from the British Isles to the Baltic."

"We'll probably get a period of bad visibility on the outside edge. I must say that just at the moment I could do with a day of low visibility and murk."


Lachmann had spent an unprofitable and sleepless night, and the dawn, which brought such good visibility, showed him a sea that was completely empty. To his angry mind, the very clarity of the weather was an added insult — as if the perfect conditions mocked his inability to make use of them.

He was loath to search the southern arc of the probable area in which his quarry lay. To do so was to admit to Braun that he had been wrong when, on the previous night, he had directed his search to the northward. But there was no help for it. It was now certain that the merchantman and destroyer had not turned north. Even so, he had not assumed that the British ships would make such a large alteration of course as they had. And so, at eight o'clock on that morning, he was actually some fifty miles northeast of the *Hecate* and her charge, and had it not been for the Focke-Wulf, it is probable that he would never have found them. At nine o'clock he was steering southeast and, left to his own devices, would have continued to search further and further to the eastward, not realizing that he had been tricked into passing ahead of the object of his search.

At nine o'clock the German U-boat Control started their morning transmission of signals, and among them was one for U-506.

"At 0805 this morning aircraft reports damaged tanker towed by destroyer in position 54° 15' N. 19° 30' W. Course 085°, speed 4 knots. No other surface escort observed. You are to close and sink this easy target forthwith."

The *Kapitän* winced as he read it. U-boat Command was laying the whip across his shoulders! Although he did not like the *Konteradmiral,* he could not understand why that officer did not appear to like him. He had to wait longer than usual at the head of the list before he had been given a command, and had even experienced the mortification of seeing a junior promoted over his head. When this occurred, he had buttressed his own mind with the thought that at some time or place he must have inadvertently angered someone who now mattered. He consoled himself with the thought that within the next twenty-four hours he would sink both ships. Then the unpleasantness with the Admiral would surely be forgotten.

Standing by his bunk, Lachmann beat the hard edge of the bunkboard with his fist. "I've got to sink them. I'm going to sink them." Catching sight of Magda's letter on the edge of the shelf, he crumpled it still more and tossed it unthinkingly to one side, where it rolled to the floor. Damn it, he couldn't even fix his thoughts on home. Only on those damned British ships that he couldn't find. They were becoming indelibly printed on the retina of his mind.

The men too were against him. Quite reasonably, they would have preferred as captain the one they had learned to trust. He hoped that in three or six months' time, when it was his turn for a rest, they'd think of him as they now thought of Weissmüller, who had been sent to the Baltic Training Flotilla. So far they had never given him a chance. And the officers, on whom he should have been able to rely, were as bad as the men. They were all in league against him! He was made to feel a stranger in his own boat — and what more could he do, or be? He needed an early success to gain control of his men — and success eluded him.

He brushed his hand across his forehead, a nervous gesture. Then, pulling himself together, he parted the curtains and went out to the control room to plot a course that would lead him to the enemy.

The course when laid off proved to be 202° and the distance forty-five miles. It would take him three hours to go the full distance, but, as he might reasonably expect to sight the surface ships fifteen miles away, he hoped to see them about eleven o'clock. Leaving orders that he was to be called at half past ten, he lay down to take what little rest he could.

His deductions had been accurate. At ten minutes to eleven the masts and funnels of both the destroyer and merchantman were in sight. That was good. But either his own aircraft had not seen the big flying boat or it had arrived after the reconnaissance plane had left. The aircraft was a very bad thing indeed. Its presence turned what should have been a simple target into one he thought was almost impossible of approach during daylight hours. He was angered still more by the knowledge that the Admiral ashore would not know of this extra hazard he had to face.

U-506 slunk once more into the protecting depths. Every now and then, from a safe distance, she inspected the British party through her periscope, but found no chance of eluding the vigilant patrol. At one o'clock she saw with relief that the Sunderland was going away, and watched. with satisfaction the signalling between ship and. plane. She was so intent on this transaction that she omitted to carry out her routine sweep for other dangers. When at last Lachmann swung the periscope around, he found himself looking at the pendulous body, straight wings and four roaring propellers of the fresh Sunderland which had, unnoticed by him, relieved the other. The U-boat only just got down to a safe depth in time. That experience did nothing to improve her captain's temper — and it was an hour before he dared risk another inspection.

With the coming of the relief aircraft it was now obvious to Lachmann that he would have to wait until dark to make his attack.

## Chapter 13

"You'll take your turn at washing-up — same as everyone else!" Pengelley thrust an armful of dirty plates, piled in a mess tin, into the reluctant hands of the outraged Sibson.

"Flip me pink if you ain't got another think coming!" Sibson had been momentarily obliged to take the metalware, but had no intention of keeping it. "Them as spends their last few hours working as cooks don't wash up — and well you knows it. This hooker ain't no flipping destroyer, and aboard this crate the 'hook' on your arm don't get you nowhere. Here! You take this lot back, Mister Leading Flipping Seaman. And, if you wants 'em washed — you washes them yourself."

Majestically the speaker poised his bulk over the smaller man, and then, his eyes piglike with anger in an unshaven face, he flung the plates back at Pengelley.

"You insubordinate bastard. You'll go in the report for this!" Pengelley's arm was drawn back, his hand clenched.

"Report, my bloody foot. You give your report to the first flipping Jerry that slams a 'fish' into us." Sibson got his blow in first. It rocked Pengelley back against the side of the wheelhouse, from which he gained support.

Pengelley leaped. His arm worked like a piston, and Sibson, who could fight but had never learned to box, went crashing backward. "While I've a badge and you ain't, you'll do as you're told."

Hart flung himself between them. Wheeler, who from outside the wheelhouse had heard the clatter of plates and the raised voices, ran to help Hart.

"Can't you silly fools behave? Haven't we got enough without fighting among ourselves?" Wheeler asked.

"Well, sir, it were like this ..." Both spoke together, and both stopped at the same time.

"I know," Wheeler said. "I don't doubt that both of you have some right on your side. But, for heaven's sake, there are too few of us to indulge in this sort of foolery."

"Them as cooks don't wash up," Sibson insisted.

The problem, small and of no real account, seemed insoluble. It was left to the tanker herself to resolve the matter. The *Antioch* managed a heavier roll than usual. The sudden unexpected motion set all four men to stagger. When they had recovered themselves, the sea and their common predicament loomed larger, personal dissension smaller.

"For this, you'll both do the washing-up for the rest of the day," Wheeler told them.

Grumbling, the two collected the plates and shuffled away.

Wheeler was left with Hart. He had come to rely on Hart, the oldest man in his crew, for keeping discipline when he himself was out of the wheelhouse. "What on earth started that off so early in the morning?"

"They're jumpy as hell, sir," Hart said. "It just blew up when my back was turned. You was out on the bridge wing at the time, and then, quicker than you can slip on a banana skin, there was Sibson and Pengelley squaring up to each other like a couple of bloody cocks on a dunghill."

"They haven't enough to keep them busy," Wheeler said. "Either there's too much to do — or too little. The Greeks left the ship in pretty good order. You can't really expect our men to get down to putting a whipping on here or renewing something there. Neither can you suggest they should chip and paint parts of someone else's ship. But if we can't keep them busy they'll talk their way into trouble."

"It may be better now, sir," Hart said, "since we found that pack of cards."

"Or worse," Wheeler said despondently. "There's nothing like cards for causing quarrels." He thought he had more than the enemy, the weather and the tow to worry about. "That Sibson's a queer devil," he said. "Good enough when it comes to work, but ..."

"He's a proper hard case, sir," Hart told him. "He's had to make his own way in the world ever since he were a kid. You can

99

always tell. He's that keen on his 'rights' there's no living with him, unless you knuckles under all the time — which isn't natural and can't be good for him. I'll have him chopping wood this morning, and when I gets back I know I'll find a bigger heap than anyone else would hack off in the time — and he'll hand me out some unpleasant remark that'll make me want to push his blasted face in. P'haps I'd better get along and see how they're doing."

Hart left, and Wheeler went out onto the bridge deck. When he had chosen his men for the *Antioch* he had every expectation of being relieved within a couple of days by a crew from the tug. Had he ever had such an experience before or had he the chance to choose again, he would have brought at least one man who could play a musical instrument — and made certain he brought it with him. And all the periodicals he could have laid hands on. The men were badly in need of something to take the place of thought. It was a bitter reflection on humanity that, even for such a comparatively short period, they could not get along without dissension. They were continually shifting friendships, forming fronts against other individuals or pairs, threatening open warfare. Just like the big world beyond, the horizon, of which they formed such an infinitesimal fraction. If his men couldn't agree, how could you expect ...? "Oh hell and blistering damnation," Wheeler said to himself, "I want to get married," and stumped down the ladder to go forward and have another look at the towing cable which he well knew he'd find in perfect order. He had been to see it only half an hour before. There was nothing else to do.

Later, just before lunch, he had left the wheelhouse to look once again at the cable. But when he was only halfway down the ladder he discovered that he had left his scarf behind. He climbed back and opened the wheelhouse door.

Sibson stood between him and the light from the far side of the house. He was showing an obviously impressed Pengelley something in a slim leather box. It was in tune with the whole of life aboard the *Antioch* that these two, whom he had so recently separated as enemies, should now be seen joined in conspiracy. Sibson, surprised, had to make two movements with his hand: one to close the box, and the next to slip it into the pocket of his duffel-coat. But Wheeler had seen the wristwatch. There was no doubt that Sibson had been rifling the cabins. The realization was a blow to the pit of his stomach.

Hastily taking his scarf from the hook, he went out onto the bridge. He had given no thought to the possibility of pilfering; and had it even crossed his mind he would have dismissed the suggestion as an unworthy reflection on his men. He now had to face the fact that if Sibson was brazen enough to disclose his action to the leading seaman, it was only because he felt entitled to the pickings. Wheeler's first reaction was to force a private showdown with Sibson. The discipline of the Service did not entirely run in his detached situation. He had no senior petty officer, and none of the panoply of command.

On the other hand, Sibson's show of pride in his success might really be due to guilt: a guilt that called for the participation of the others. Then, even if their joining him should reduce the size of his booty, Sibson would at least have the moral support of his companions for having what he held. On this view of the situation, they would all have to be tackled together — before the rot had spread too far. It was a disease which, once started, might spread very fast.

Had he not returned unexpectedly, it was probable he'd never have made the discovery. The ship was so vast, and there were so many places where valuables could be hidden. No customs officer would ever search men who had been put aboard in mid-ocean. By ignoring the whole thing he could keep his men together until the tow was finished. And temptation even suggested to him that such employment would keep them happily engaged.

But to overlook theft was not really possible. He saw the problem, reduced to its three dimensions, as in reality a challenge to himself. There was no other way of looking at it, for if he failed himself he would feel that he had no right to the stripes on his arm — nor, for that matter, to Anne. He wondered how Murrell would have faced the situation? It was quite certain that if he had put the question to the *Hecate's* captain, Murrell would have said, "Go in and tackle the lot." He also knew that Murrell would, inside himself, have felt just as insecure over the matter as he did. This knowledge went a long way to give him confidence. For encouragement he told himself that any man so sure of himself that he felt no qualms would probably not have enough imagination to see the situation as a whole.

It was time for the men to gather in the wheelhouse for their dinner. He watched Hart stumble forward from the galley bearing a huge mess tin covered with a cloth. As it was carried past him, Wheeler could smell the unmistakable odour of macaroni and cheese. Trotman and Anders came forward too and went into the house. They had spent the forenoon cleaning the Oerlikon and Bofors guns. All the men were now inside except White, who was keeping watch on the weather wing of the bridge.

Wheeler thought, "It's now or never. It can't be never — so it must be now." He called to White, "Come inside for a moment. I want to talk to the lot of you."

He held the door for the signalman, followed him in, and shut it. There was a pleasant haze of tobacco smoke, and a wonderful smell of hot food from the big mess tin which stood on the armour-plate shelter that had been fitted as a wartime measure around the steering wheel. There was a general hum of conversation. His entry had apparently disturbed no one.

Two or three of the shutters had been taken down to admit the daylight. From where he stood he could look along the whole fore part of the ship. The sea showed blue through the scupper holes which pierced her bulwarks. Over the ellipse of the bows he could see the struggling destroyer. The waves astern of her were churned white by the propellers, and her tattered white ensign flew from the stump mainmast. He distilled strength for himself from the sight of his own ship, and, drawing himself up to his full height, he fired his first broadside.

"I want to speak to you all. There's something very serious to be said." The men, caught unawares, faced him, their expressions varying through all grades of surprise. There was no possibility of going back now. "I know that one man has been pilfering the cabins," Wheeler told them. "That is entirely against the custom of the Navy. Though I have authority, I have little power to exercise it aboard this ship. I can only ask those who haven't taken anything to

102

help me deal with the situation." He paused for breath, to let the words sink in and to watch what reaction they might have produced.

Sibson had half turned away. His shoulders, hunched, suggested truculence. Pengelley looked down at his feet. Anders appeared to be completely mystified, as if he did not quite understand what was taking place. The pause had gone on longer than Wheeler expected. But he felt the breaking power of silence at work. He thought he could afford to wait. Sibson, broken by it, himself broke it. "So what? So I took a watch — and why the hell not? The bloody Greeks have hopped it, haven't they? It's not them that are risking their flipping lives, it's us. I reckon it's cheap at the price! If we was doing this in peacetime, we'd get salvage money — thousands 'a quid apiece. What'll we get out of this lot if we don't help ourselves but a bloody great bonfire. We're plain daft if we don't take some payment in advance." He grinned behind tight lips. "Findings is keepings, ain't they?" He turned to the others with a gesture that assumed their support.

The atmosphere was tense. Some of the men were on Sibson's side. Wheeler could feel it. Pengelley was one. He came from Cornwall. His forebears had been smugglers and wreckers — and considered none the worse for that. White too was a waverer. As if the idea had only just presented itself to his imagination, he looked like a child brought face to face with a bran tub into which he might not now be allowed to plunge his hand. And even Hart was considering the question. He had not, as Wheeler hoped, dismissed Sibson's plea at once.

Help came from an unexpected quarter. "No, Sibby," Trotman said, "you done us all wrong. Thieving at sea won't never bring you luck — and you know it. Blimey, you'd steal the milk from a blind baby, you would."

"Trust you to put your bloody foot in it." Sibson turned on Trotman. But the morning's short scrap, in which Sibson had learned to respect the strength of a smaller man, had its effect on him now. Trotman was too big to bully. The suggestion that fate might not be blind — worse still, that retribution might follow wrongdoing — struck hard at men living in momentary fear of a dreadful death. The inconsistency of acting on two principles troubled none of them, for they made no attempt to analyze the motives on which decision was based. Wheeler saw that the appeal to ineradicable magic had had more effect than anything he could have said. Again he waited.

"I ain't no bloody pirate." Hart moved restlessly towards the mess tin, where the orange-brown skin on the surface showed signs of shrivelling as the food cooled.

"Anders?" Wheeler asked inquiringly.

"Sir?" the blond seaman answered.

"What do you think?" Wheeler repeated.

"I dunno, sir. Don't rightly know what it's all about."

"Sibson took a watch from one of the officers' cabins," Wheeler told him. "He thinks that, because there's no salvage money, he's entitled to it."

"Ooh," Anders said, "he can't do that — that's stealing."

There was a burst of laughter, and with that Sibson's support vanished.

"Aren't you the bright boy?" Sibson spat at Anders.

Wheeler crossed to Sibson, who was left standing alone. "I'll take care of it, Sibson," he said and held out his hand, able to meet the angry glance with assurance.

For a moment Sibson hesitated. Then his hand went to his pocket. "Okay, you win," he said.

"Like the cable — not to be mentioned again," Wheeler said, and: "Now for heaven's sake let's have our dinner before it gets cold."


Since eleven o'clock that morning Murrell had felt sure that a U-boat had joined the party. It was a particularly nasty sensation, for, however efficient the U-boat might believe the destroyer's asdic to be, he knew that there was a large arc astern where, because of the disturbance caused by her own propellers and by the *Antioch,* the machine could not detect the enemy.

Normally this arc would have been covered in the process of zigzagging. But on a steady course he was vulnerable all the time from astern. The U-boat had only to attack from there to make certain of a kill. Murrell's only hopes were that the opposing captain would not realize this, that he would credit the asdic with greater efficiency than it possessed, or be kept at a safe distance by the escorting aircraft.

It was during this time of comparative immunity for the leading ship and greater danger to the tanker that his concern for Wheeler's safety reached a maximum. His mind, although repeatedly told to be quiet, kept calling from memory events which had occurred in two years of sailing together. The decision which had put Wheeler aboard the tanker had greatly increased his own burden.

The doctor, . coming to relieve the Captain and asking his usual, "How is she?" received the answer, "Bloody."

"Trying to go any particular way?" Macmillan made another attempt, only to have the telephone thrust at him.

"No," Murrell said and turned away.

The doctor smoothed his chin with his hand and twisted down one corner of his mouth — a grimace that made him look like a dissatisfied gnome. His eyes followed the Captain's back as he roughly pushed past a lookout on his way to the compass platform.

Murrell went down to his cabin deeply vexed by his own ill-humour. Acknowledging the cause, he sought to minimize its effect on innocent and defenceless men by removing himself from their presence.

Then, just as he was finishing his lunch, came the signal from the relief aircraft, "U-boat at periscope depth four miles 350° from you," and presentiment was confirmed as fact. In the circumstances, there could be no sleep for him that afternoon — nor, for that matter, for any of the Hecates. He prided himself on his ability to sleep whenever he had the chance — an attribute it was essential to learn if any man was to stand the strain of years at sea. But now all he could do was to lie awake in his self-imposed seclusion with every nerve and muscle at the ready, counting the rivets on the bulkhead while he waited for the explosion or the call from the bridge that would tell him his enemy had moved in closer.

At four o'clock he went up to the bridge and made a signal to the *Antioch:* "Anticipate enemy will attack tonight. Intend to slip tow as soon as he is detected. Don't worry, only two hundred more miles." He had the signal passed by semaphore by a signalman standing in the shelter of the after house to White, who had been told to come forward into the bows of the *Antioch* to read it. He felt it safer to take precautions over such a signal, for a lamp could have been read by the U-boat if he happened to have his periscope up at the time.

During the afternoon the wind had eased. The crests of the waves, which had curled forward and broken, now loitered and lolloped back; they sank down into circular patches of dark blue flecked with white, and the splash they made could be heard on the bridge. The cumulus clouds of the morning had gone, but a thin gray film had crept over the sky from the east. With the coming of darkness their aircraft left them.

Through the thin cloud layer the stars shone with a reduced brilliance, and because their light was interfered with they appeared both larger and closer. Against this back cloth the dark spire of the destroyer's mast, with its crossed signal yards and many halyards and shrouds, moved restlessly.

The men too, who thought that the night would provide the climax of their effort, were silent. The normal chatter and laughter was absent and they moved quietly and watchfully. The routine orders could be heard more clearly than usual. The whine of the big fans that kept the boiler rooms under pressure was a constant burden that now was an irritation, where normally it soothed. On that night hearing, as well as sight, was stretched to the utmost.

Murrell had sent for the Petty Officer Radar Mechanic, and having made sure that the set was working at maximum efficiency, he explained the position. "Within the next four hours the U-boat that has been chasing us will attack. As soon as you can get him on the radar, I shall slip the tow and go after him. I'd rather go to a false alarm than have him surface and sink the *Antioch* before I can get at him. So for heaven's sake report everything. I rely on you to see your operators don't let up for a second. We'll have very little time to spare."

With that, and the loading of star shell into the guns, Murrell felt that everything had been done that could be anticipated. He went down to the heads, and, passing the open door of the forward mess deck, he saw that no hammocks had yet been slung and that the men off watch, having had their tea, were lolling about smoking and talking. On the way back to the bridge he went into the wireless office. "Lawrence — connect up the intercom for me, will you, please." Then he went up to the bridge. "I'll take her in a minute; I just want to talk to the men on the intercom," he said to the doctor as he passed.

"Hecates." He spoke into the mouthpiece when Lawrence had reported it correct. "Hecates — you're all hanging around waiting — so you might as well go to your action stations. Take plenty of warm clothing with you. I'll sound the alarm gong as usual when I want you to stand by — but if you're ready, at least we'll save a few minutes."

He went back to the doctor. "I'll take her."

"I'm all right," Macmillan said.

"But you've been conning her since half past twelve, and it's six o'clock now."

"And will you go and get some sleep too, if I do, sir?"

"No — obviously I can't."

"Then I'm quite all right until this party is over. Kirby will bring me up some sandwiches and coffee. After all, I can do this now so that I don't know whether I'm awake or asleep — and when I do go to sleep I'm sure I keep on giving helm orders. Excuse me. Starboard ten: slow port."

"Well, if you can do it, perhaps it *is* better," the Captain admitted as he went slowly back to the standard compass.

Waiting for the other side to open the battle was not a pleasant pastime. At the moment the initiative lay entirely with the U-boat. It must be wrested back as soon as the enemy showed himself.

## Chapter 14

To the northwest of the Bay of Biscay the Operations Room of the German U-boat Command had been dug deep into the hills behind the submarine base of Lorient. To this controlling brain telephones led from the Naval Ministry in Berlin, the headquarters of Reconnaissance Group 40 at Bordeaux, to the wireless station and to the many local headquarters of police, army and air force. In the centre of the room a big plot, some ten feet square, represented the whole of the North Atlantic. On this grid-lined chart coloured counters and plaques showed the positions, estimated or reported, of every U-boat and, of course, of every Allied convoy or group of ships that Naval Intelligence and Reconnaissance Wing could find.

At first the episode of Lachmann's tanker had been no more than a routine sinking. On the following morning, when the reconnaissance aircraft had taken a quick look at the convoy, it had confirmed the tanker's absence. Then Lachmann's triumph had been assumed: the sinking had been claimed and passed to the ministry in Berlin for propaganda purposes. The next day Magda was pleased and mollified to see her husband's name in print — even if it was in a very small paragraph. So far the affair gave no indication of being anything but a small local and personal success.

That this tiny seed should grow into a great tree was due to strange chances — chances which are always ready to flourish in time of war. On the morning when Lachmann's name appeared in the paper, Hans Edelman and Richter, far out in the Atlantic, were peering through the rain-drenched perspex nose of their aircraft, and a man, incongruous in civilian clothes, was standing beside the plot in *Konteradmiral* von Fichte's headquarters at Lorient. He stood, a detached observer because none of the officers present thought it politic to be seen in friendly contact with him: a journalist, who had arrived unexpectedly the night before with personal papers signed by Goebbels himself.

Behind this sudden appearance lay matters of national importance. The German papers had recently been complaining — not without justice — that the assessment of damage done to the enemy was not always substantiated by fact. Ships claimed to have been sunk had an awkward habit of reappearing on the oceans, only to be claimed sunk again with no more success than had attended the first effort. And simple addition and subtraction would prove that the air claims had been greatly exaggerated. Mathematically, the British should by now have no fighter planes left — and this was demonstrably untrue. The fact that these jibes at two of their armed services should be allowed to appear in the papers of Hitler's Reich suggested that Goebbels was behind the matter, and there were many in the senior ranks of the Navy and Luftwaffe who could speak of the fury with which Grand-Admiral Doenitz and *Reichsmarschall* Goering had accepted these editorial taunts.

Now to the Admiral's intense annoyance, Herr Spichern had come to see — or been sent to discover — how the service reports were verified before they were released. And, almost beyond belief, his attitude suggested that he intended to remain at the side of the plot throughout the unofficial but very important morning conference.

It was all the more regrettable that the signal from Richter's aircraft should arrive in the middle of the routine discussion. Holding the unwelcome message in his hands, the Admiral saw only two roads open. The first was to make a joke of the whole matter and to use this occurrence to point out to the visitor how terribly difficult it was for one side to prove any damage to the other. The alternative course was to ensure that the tanker was properly sunk, and so convert conjecture into established fact.

That there was a third choice — to make the explanation *and* arrange the tanker's end — did not occur to him because he had already taken a personal dislike to the dog-faced little civilian. He was by nature a man of action, not words. He asked for a pad and, most unusually, wrote the signal himself. In his anger he underlined the last phrase: *"You are to close the position and sink her. Repeat sink her,"* and quite ignored the fact that underlinings could not be transmitted over the wireless.

Even so, Lachmann, hundreds of miles away, had sensed the Admiral's personality behind the signal — a not-uncommon occurrence when blame is being levelled. Admirals have a latitude to write their signals in phraseology that betrays the signal's origin.

It had of course been beyond the Admiral's power to prevent the unwelcome news reaching all those around the plot, if only because the position of the damaged tanker had at once been marked with a yellow plaque. Herr Spichern, his journalist's nose sensing a scoop, looked like a setter pointing game. He said, "It is to be hoped, Herr Admiral, that you will be able to take that yellow disc away." In saying that he risked an open rupture. But it was a carefully calculated risk. He did not think the highly disciplined man would really break in public. It was amusing to let these stiff-necked sailors feel his civilian power.

The Admiral snorted — and blew his nose to hide even this small crack in his control. Already he regretted that he had not taken the first course and explained the difficulties more fully to the inquisitor. He saw himself being forced into providing a perfect case of the over-optimistic claim. As a seaman, intensely loyal to his seniors and his service, he had the greatest distrust of politicians — with whom he linked all journalists. He had no more wish to be the personal scapegoat than that any miscalculation on his part should bring odium on the naval hierarchy. It was now absolutely necessary that the Navy — in this case personified by Lachmann — should complete the job. Otherwise . . . well, he didn't care to dwell on the "otherwise." With Nazi politicians infiltrated into all levels of command he could expect no clemency from his seniors.

But when he had escaped the scrutiny of Spichern — for whom his Chief of Staff had arranged a busy day of sightseeing — the mental climate was better for cool consideration. It then seemed that Lachmann's was not so difficult a mission. A damaged tanker escorted by only a single destroyer should be an easy target. If the escort were to circle the tanker at a radius of one mile, it would take her, at cruising speed and zigzagging, more than half an hour to complete the circle — and very much longer if she were to choose a wider radius. Lachmann, on the surface at night, should have plenty of time. Von Fichte felt sure that by the following day this particular worry would have been solved and his fears for his own career proved groundless.

But the next morning, at half past eight, it was known that the destroyer was even more handicapped than they had supposed. She was trying to tow the tanker herself. The Admiral wrote another signal to U-506 — and this time no officer in the plot thought it odd that anyone so senior should write his own signals. The atmosphere was charged with drama that centred on the yellow plaque on the black plot. Spichern's well-drilled face was a mask of deferential interest that no one could fault. But even so, his attitude could not hide a pleased intensity that rallied all the officers there in defence of their chief.

"... *No other surface escort observed. You are to close and sink this easy target forthwith.*" Von Fichte flung the pad on the table and, making a sign to the Chief of Staff to follow him, strode into his office.

"What are we going to do with him?" he asked. And the Chief of Staff had no doubt to whom his Admiral referred. It was Spichern, not Lachmann, who was the object of both their thoughts.

"He's been shown all there is to see here. Can we not give him some other hare to chase? How about loaning him to the Luftwaffe for the day?"

"Make it a day and a night," the Admiral. growled, "and it's an excellent idea. You'll have to sell it to the little runt first, then get on to Air Command Northwest. Let me know as soon as he's clear of the base. I can't breathe with that man about!" Von Fichte ran his finger between his collar and a neck where the skin was hot and moist.

But the Air General, who could find no excuse to refuse the unwelcome guest during the day, had no intention of extending his hospitality over the night. Did the Navy not know how very cramped they were for accommodation? Even his own officers were sleeping in quarters that no decent German dog would tolerate! Herr Spichern would be returned to his present hosts by midnight — or earlier.

Which meant, of course, as soon as the Air General could get rid of him. And with that von Fichte would have to be content.

"Then, for the love of heaven, keep him out of my sight!" the Admiral exclaimed when told of the only partial success; and added perplexedly, "You'd think there'd be more interservice cooperation than there is." A member of the elder service, he could never understand the assumption of omnipotence on the part of the Luftwaffe officers with the new weapon. "Self-styled little gods!" he said, and again the Chief of Staff understood just what the Admiral meant.

## Chapter 15

Lachmann brought U-506 to the surface with deliberation. If he had been over-hasty when, four nights before, he had last had the tanker in his sights, he was not going to make the same mistake again.

From where he had chosen to surface, four thousand yards on the starboard bow of the target, he could see the long bulk of the tanker quite plainly and make out with only a little strain the slighter form of the destroyer. In the prevailing conditions of light — it was only very rarely that it was completely dark at sea — there was no chance of his being seen at that range, and so no need to keep the boat running at "reduced buoyancy," when only the conning tower was above the water. He gave the order that brought his boat to full surface trim.

In the better weather the seas had lost their vice, and at the low speeds that were all that would be necessary to deal with such a slow-moving target, the conning tower would be quite free of spray when he had fully surfaced. He had only to satisfy himself that the attack which he had planned would work, and then carry it out. If it proved impracticable, he could either stay where he was and work out another, or else dive again and take his time. He was in no hurry. And, even if the wind was more chill than he had expected, he had just enough clothes on to prevent the cold from interfering with his efficiency in the comparatively short time he intended to stay on the surface. He had the whole night before him. This time his opponent could pull no surprise. She was a sitting duck. In fact, the target was better than that. It was a brace of ducks. The destroyer added to the tanker would surely appease the Admiral.

He grasped the rail with gloved hands and allowed the sensation of omnipotence to seep into his mind. He was all alone on the bridge and, for the moment, happy to be so. Because he had not known for how long he would keep his boat in cruising trim — he would certainly take her back to reduced buoyancy before firing —

he had not sent down for the bridge crew. He did not see how they could have helped, and two more men in the conning tower would only increase the time needed to dive if he had to. He found pleasure in being up there on the windy deck, the sole guardian of his ship's safety and the brain that controlled her power to destroy.

Leaning over the side of the conning tower, his glasses fixed on the tanker, he tried to estimate her length. One hundred and thirty meters, and the tow line as much again — or possibly a little more, say one hundred and sixty meters. The destroyer one hundred and ten meters. She did not look it, but the target she made for the underwater weapons was almost as big as that of the tanker itself. In the improving condition of the sea, he intended to set the torpedoes to a shallow depth in the case of both ships. Two torpedoes would be angled to hit each vessel. He would only need to give one order, and his mission would be complete.

But first he would move in closer to the target. There was no need to stay out at four thousand meters. He could make a certainty of the job by shortening the range by half. He would drop back from his present position, which was forty-five degrees on the bow, to one that was something nearer to eighty degrees. With this very slow target there was no need to take the more usual bow shot: the nearer his approach to a beam attack, the greater the effective length of the target. He was going to make sure. He had already wasted four torpedoes on the contraption that the British had set afloat the night before. That was going to take some explaining away. He felt hot under the collar — really felt the hot blood rising — each time the memory returned to his mind. And he was thinking about it now, wasting time.

Clattering feet on the ladder that led from the control room below brought his mind back to the present and an engine-room artificer to the conning tower. The newcomer saluted Lachmann. "Herr .*Kapitän,* the Herr Engineer requires a tin of hydraulic oil from the casing locker. I request permission to get it."

"If you must," Lachmann grumbled. "Though you may tell the Herr Engineer...." No. Now that he was a commanding officer, men could not be used to carry that sort of message to another officer. He would have to wait to tell the Engineer himself what he thought of him for not obtaining all the necessary stores before they had dived in the morning.

The man swung himself down to the deck and made his way aft. There he raised a heavy cover that was let into the wooden deck planking. Below was a locker, open to the sea, where imperishable stores could be carried. The drums were securely lashed, and Voss glanced rather dubiously at the conning tower before he clambered into the locker to undo the fastenings of the drum he had been sent to fetch.

Lachmann passed the information that he had gained of their targets down the voice pipe to Gessner at the attack-table. He made that officer repeat back each number to him. He was going to stick to every single item of the drill that he had been taught in the course for commanding officers.


Murrell, after hanging around the bridge for an hour while the doctor conned the ship, had tried the seclusion of his sea-cabin. But even here he could find no relief from the agony of waiting. Finally, he moved himself to that position where the first news of the enemy's presence would be known — the Radar Office.

But before going down there, he had been back to the bridge. "I'm going down to the Radar Office," he had told Graves. And then to the doctor, "I'll be in the Radar Office if you want me."

"Like a cat on hot bricks," Graves commented down his telephone to the doctor.

"So would you be if you were carrying his load," Macmillan replied. "Starboard ten: stop starboard." And then after giving the order he had gone on, "Why not try letting him carry yours too — it won't make much difference to his, and it might help you with your own."

Graves was surprised that the doctor had detected his apprehension. He had hoped it had not shown. But then, he thought, everyone else was the same — jumpy.

In the close air of the dark and ill-ventilated Radar Office Murrell stood behind the operator. He supported himself by a hand over his head, and his body, heavy in its duffel-coat, swung in time to the ship's roll. The petty officer on the set slowly spun the wheel that sent the searching beam around and around. A radar mechanic sat beside him. On the scan, the pencil of light traced its continual pattern. The cable that turned the aerial rattled a little in its sheath. It was the only sound in the hut, from which all noise of the ship had been shuttered. There were no sea sounds, and no sough of the wind.

For a captain used to the open bridge it was a strange sensation to be enclosed within clipped doors. Stranger still to be so separated from his officers. The eerie green light from the set was reflected- on the faces of the three men. Too weak to penetrate the shadows, it lay like varnish on the facial planes. To each other, had they been able to tear their eyes from the set, they would have looked already dead.

"There! What's that?" the Captain said.

The beam of the set wavered and then swung back. It passed beyond the tiny spot of brighter fluorescence, retraced its path, then hovered over it. The spot grew in intensity. Its outlines- hardened. The watchers' breathing deepened. "Onions!" Murrell thought, distracted. "He would have to eat onions tonight!"

"Bearing green four-eight. Range oh-four-oh." The operator spoke with maddening slowness. Aware of the importance, he was making doubly sure of each figure.

Murrell, impatient for certainty, had to fight hard to restrain his voice. "What do you make of it?" he asked.

"Could be, sir." The man was noncommittal. With his captain there he could not be expected to take the responsibility of making a definite classification.

With a shock Murrell realized this. Calling instinct to his aid he recognized in the bright little spot his enemy. He called up the voice pipe to the bridge. "Captain here. Slip the tow. As soon as she's free, steer one-one-three degrees at full speed. I'm coming up now."


"Christ!" Trotman strained his eyes into the darkness. "She's gorn!" He ran into the wheelhouse to call the others. "The *Hecate's* gone! She's slipped the flipping tow and gone!"

116

His shout through the door brought them all scuffling to their feet. Then he ran back to the bridge, leaving the door swinging to the ship's roll, which, now that there was no longer a steady pull from the destroyer, had markedly increased.

Wheeler, telling himself that an officer should not rush about with the men, tried to go more slowly, but arrived at the same time. Huddled together in the little shelter on the starboard wing of the bridge they stood and looked into the black night. "Where is she now?" Wheeler asked.

"Can't see anything of her," Hart answered. "Nothing but waves an' more waves."

"Trotman," Wheeler asked, "which way did she turn?"

"I dunno, sir. One minute she was there — as she's always been –then she weren't there any longer."

White began to sing. His voice above the noise of wind and water was thin. *"Lord hear us when we call to Thee, for those in peril ... "* There was the sound of flesh on flesh, and a wail that ended in a sob. In the dark and the press of bodies, it was as certain that only one knew who had struck the blow as that no one else would ever try to discover who it had. been.

Hart, speaking over-quickly, said, "It's a nice little house in a row. Nothing fancy — but the woodwork's pretty decent. They knew how to build houses in them days."

Anders was heard to ask for a quart of mixed — with the froth on top. Sibson said aloud, "Up the flipping creek — up the flipping creep without a paddle. That's us."

Wheeler thought of the ordered hustle and scurry there would be in the destroyer before the *Hecate* settled down to "action stations." Once their ship had slipped the tow, her men would be freed. They'd feel comparatively safe. She would no longer be part of the target. There was only one target now; the deck beneath his feet lurched as it rolled.

## Chapter 16

It took Lachmann some time to deal with Voss, and to give the unhurried details of the targets to Gessner. Four minutes passed before he was free to look at the tanker. At the now-reduced range, she was easier to see. For a full minute he studied her carefully. She was a big modern vessel — a really worthwhile victim. Perhaps, with luck, he would find something in her wreckage that would tell him her name. It was always so much more rewarding to be able to put that in the signal. He swung his binoculars slowly towards the destroyer's position. Then, in bewilderment, back again to the tanker. His heart beat furiously. Its hectic pulsing made his hand shake.

There was no need for the glasses to see the destroyer. He roared, "Full ahead" down the voice pipe, and turned to look again at the horror that bore down on him. There was no time, no opportunity, to wonder how it had happened. Enough that she was less than five hundred meters away, and travelling so fast that as she rolled to windward the bow wave was massed in an arch of foam that rose higher than the tearing bows.

Then U-506 was leaping ahead herself. By instinct Lachmann turned his stern towards the enemy.

Moving twice as fast as the submarine, the destroyer was closing rapidly. He thought he could even hear the roar of her bow wave.

The enemy was dead astern — one hundred meters. With voice surprisingly calm he ordered the wheel hard aport, and, having closed the voice-pipe vent, his finger pressed the button that set the klaxon roaring. Then he stepped calmly into the hatch, paused a moment to see that his own stern was swinging widely, and went on down, knowing that the turning circle of his own boat was so much smaller than the destroyer's that she could not possibly carry out her intention to ram. He was thankful he had not lost his nerve. He

118

turned the wheel that locked the hatch and dropped lightly to the deck of the control room.

The boat's bow was depressed steeply. The clatter of the diesels had been replaced by the whir of the electric motors; and for the moment the dive was, except for the corkscrew motion, just like any other of the emergency dives that U-506 had made in her two years of life.

"Hard aport." Murrell's command could be heard by all on the bridge.

With the thirty-four-thousand horsepower of her twin turbines striving to push her beyond the thirty-three knots of her designed speed, the *Hecate* lay over sharply as her rudder bit deep into the sea, and Murrell had to grip the binnacle firmly to prevent himself being catapulted from the platform. Men went slithering and falling on the wet decks, while, in an effort to see the ram take place, they hectically tried to recover their footing.

But Murrell knew that the U-boat would not be rammed, and that all he had achieved by his rapid pounce had been to wrest the initiative from the enemy's grasp. With the U-boat a fugitive below the surface, it was an advantage that he hoped to retain.

Sliding sideways into the waves that broke clean across her low deck, the destroyer turned desperately. But all the time she was passing outside the more quickly turning U-boat. Like a swimmer carried away by a strong tide, the diving U-boat eluded all her efforts to catch it.

"Half ahead both. One-five-oh revolutions. Steer oh-three-oh. Lower the asdic. Start transmissions. Search the port side." The orders rolled mechanically from Murrell's tongue.

"Quarterdeck reports a man in the water, sir. They've dropped a flare." The Yeoman had answered the telephone.

"What a time to fall overboard! I can't possibly stop for him now," the Captain exclaimed — real worry creasing his forehead.

"Not one of ours, sir. Some joker must 'a got left behind when she dived — they said he weren't half kicking up a fuss."

"Oh well, that's different. Not that I'm hard-hearted, but he can wait until we've finished with his pals."

"Echo bearing red eight-five. Submarine. Range six hundred." Graves' voice, full of satisfaction, rose from the voice pipe that led to the asdic hut.

"Thank you, Graves. Are you ready to attack?"

"Ready to attack, sir."

Turning to port, the destroyer had now changed places with her adversary. At reduced speed she stalked sedately over the waves in quest of her prey.

U-506, after her scrambled dive, had some difficulty in regaining trim. She twisted and turned like a porpoise below the water, while her well-drilled crew fought for a control that they never quite lost. Within five minutes she had settled down to a steady course eighty meters below the surface. Her motors turned pleasantly. The air in the boat had recently been renewed. Looking around him, Lachmann, until he remembered Voss, was well satisfied at his escape. That memory was not so good, and even though every man in the boat knew that the same fate could overtake any of them in an emergency, it would need a lot of explaining to the Engineer. In Lachmann's own mind the sense of blame was really brought by the fact that, in the excitement of evading the destroyer, he had truly forgotten the unfortunate man.

"Destroyer approaching starboard beam," the voice pipe from the hydrophone cabinet announced. Lachmann, who, when he had been an executive officer under a captain, had experienced this before, found it a less nerve-wracking proceeding than previously. In command, he had the thinking to do, and this left no time for fear to gnaw at his vitals.

He decided to turn away under full helm. Even when he was below the water, he could still turn more quickly than the destroyer. The steady beat of the destroyer's propellers was heard plainly, but the sensation of his boat turning under helm was satisfying, and presently the propellers were heard to pass down the starboard side. Depth charges began to explode, but although they shook the

120

submarine and some lamps were broken, they were too far away to do any material damage.

Twice Lachmann had escaped the single destroyer by making full use of his manoeuvrability. He was confident that he could keep it up. Down the voice pipe that led to the hydrophone cabinet he said, "Tell me when the destroyer turns, and then at once give me a bearing."

*"Jawohl, Herr Kapitän."*

They waited in strained silence; forty men in a steel shell that was suspended in the sea, held there by delicate machinery, controlled by their own nerves.

The Engineer appeared in the doorway. He was excited. *"Herr Kapitän. Herr Kapitän,"* he said.

"Yes?" Lachmann guessed what was coming.

"Voss!" the Engineer accused.

"He has been unfortunate."

"You mean ...?" the Engineer said. Lachmann nodded.

"That is bad." The Engineer spoke grimly.

"It was his own fault. You know...."

"Destroyer approaching starboard beam," the voice pipe announced, "bearing green eight-five to green nine-oh."

But Lachmann was busy defending himself. "... You know the orders!"

"Of course, *Herr Kapitän*, I know the orders, and I know too that it is something which very rarely happens!" The Engineer spoke with bitter anger and without respect.

"Are you challenging my judgment?" Lachmann's voice rose as anger answered anger.

Braun touched the Captain's sleeve. *"Herr Kapitän.* The destroyer!" he said.

"What! Why has it not been reported?" Lachmann spun around.

"It was, *Herr Kapitän,"* Braun said defensively.

"What was the report?"

"Starboard beam."

"Hard aport."

The dead silence in the control room was broken by the steady thrumming beat that all could hear. Like a train passing over an iron bridge, the confident propellers swept above them.

They waited, and while they waited the ten heavy canisters sank down towards them.

The ten depth charges began to explode — not all together, but in pairs. The stricken boat was flung backwards and forwards, from side to side, and up and down, by the successive pressure waves. For one mad moment her bow reared, and then hung down — the angle increasing all the time. Every light bulb had been smashed and only the dim glow of the emergency lighting enabled the terror-stricken men to see their equally horrified companions. And even when the dreadful explosions had ceased, the boat, as high-pressure air escaped from broken pipes and great bubbles rose from her torn flanks, went on shivering.

To save himself from falling, Lachmann had seized the ladder that led to the conning tower. But now, as her bow dipped, his feet lost their grip. Men and gear fell forward and past him and landed in a heap against the forward bulkhead. One or two, because they could not help themselves, went on through the doorway that led to the fore part of the boat.

From forward came a dreadful hissing, as sea water entered the batteries, and despairing moans rose to Lachmann's ears as he hung by his arms from the ladder. The water was rising now, coming up into the control room through the door to which Lachmann's own feet pointed. It was foul and bubbling water that made the hanging man cough and retch. He felt the wetness at his feet, and around his middle. Before his face a letter floated on the fetid tide — the ink was already becoming smudged with the water, but Lachmann could read "why have you not had your leave?"

Then mercifully the sides of the boat collapsed, for she had already long since passed the depth to which a submarine may safely dive.


"Breaking-up noises." Graves's voice came from the asdic hut.

122

"What was that attack like?" the Captain asked the Navigator, who was down below on the plot.

"Copybook, sir! That time I don't think he knew it was coming. He never altered course."

Slowly the *Hecate* nosed her way over the position. There was a strong smell of diesel oil, and bubbles rose steadily to the surface in a constant stream.

"Let's go and see if our lucky lad's still there," Murrell said. "We can't be very far away. Port twenty. Steady on one-eight-oh."

The doctor came up beside him. "Gosh! That lot of pills really was worth a guinea a box."

"Feeling a little stronger?" Murrell laughed.

"Now that Jerry has been removed from the immediate scene I'm feeling a lot happier! He wasn't a very nice bedfellow when we were towing."

"Light in the water. Fine on the starboard bow." A lookout reported it.

"I can see it," Murrell answered, and to the wheelhouse, "Steer one-nine-oh. Slow both."

They found Voss. "Cor, sir, you couldn't help but find 'im — bleating like a bleeding goat he were, sir." Leading Seaman Thomas brought the news from the quarterdeck.

"Doctor, you can speak German, can't you?"

"I spent a year at Bonn University."

"I thought so. Then will you go down below and find out what you can? First, I want to know the U-boat's number. It looks so much better to give it in the first signal. Nice and tidy. Then try and find out if there are any more of its pals about — and anything else you can think of. Take the bridge messenger down with you and send him back with the number written down on a piece of paper."

The Captain watched the doctor's muffled form move towards the ladder. Reaction from excitement set in, and tiredness and the increasing cold overwhelmed him like a wave. "Half ahead together, one-two-oh revolutions. Coxswain. Pipe 'Secure' and 'Both watches lay aft to recover tow.' "

"Yeoman, make to *Antioch* by blue light; 'U-boat sunk. One survivor. I am going to attempt to recover tow now.' When you've sent that one, bring me a pad and I'll make a signal to the Commander-in-Chief."

From Voss they learned the U-boat's number and that, as far as he knew, U-506 had been the only boat in the vicinity. They also heard from him of the abortive attack on the raft, and that information gave Murrell the greatest pleasure, particularly the quite-unexpected panic that the two tins had caused.

Murrell wrote out the signal. "C-in-C Western Approaches from *Hecate*. Have sunk U-506 in position 54° 30' N. 18° 05' W. One survivor. Am recovering tow."

The doctor had joined him after the interrogation. It had not taken long, for Voss had been only too ready to talk to someone who spoke his language so fluently. "You go and get your head down. I've had a rest, if not a sleep, since you have. And I've got to recover the tow."

"Really, sir?"

"Yes, Doc, and thanks a lot for your help. Honestly, I just don't know what I'd have done without you."

"Well, thank you for the thrill, sir," Macmillan said.

"Thrill?"

"Good heavens, yes."

"What bloodthirsty chaps you medicos are! I hate that side of war. Such a pity that we can't knock the ships from under the men, and let it go at that."

"You don't think the German captain thought that way, do you?"

"For all I know he may have done. That's the trouble — but he'd have sunk us just the same. Perhaps that's what makes war so bloody silly. We're getting near the *Antioch* now. Goodnight, Doc. I'll see you at four."

Slowly and carefully Murrell took the *Hecate* stern-first toward the bow of the *Antioch*. One hour and ten minutes later the tow was under way again.

## Chapter 17

During the night the cloud layer gradually thickened until it extinguished the stars. Dawn of the fourth day of their ordeal came slowly and brought an intensification of the already-hard horizon.

For a considerable distance from the ships the water had the sheen of silver, but as it neared the horizon it became a band of gray that was even darker than the leaden-hued sky above. As though the sea and sky had changed places, the ships floated like specks in a circle of light under a cloud that had the solidity of a sheet of metal. The wind, fitful and light, was more seen than felt in the little cat's-paws that chased one another over the silken surface. Colour existed only in the froth of the destroyer's wake, which, tinged and spiralled with the palest green, reached out as far as the stem of the *Antioch*. There it divided, one half flowing past each side of the bluff bow.

They had lost the advantage of the strong westerly wind which had hurried them home, but they had the better behaviour of the *Antioch* in the calmer sea to set against its loss. Although the cloud had made it impossible for Masters to take a star-sight that morning, they had in the last twenty-four hours made by dead reckoning another hundred and two miles, and were left with only one hundred and eight to go.

In the weather conditions that morning a sighting between aircraft and ships would be made at a very great distance. The Focke-Wulf came especially to inspect them. Watching the German plane, Morrell spoke over his shoulder to the doctor. "This morning it has a surprised and worried look."

"He's much closer today than he was yesterday," Macmillan agreed. "Probably he can't believe his own eyes."

"Coming in to make sure," Murrell said. "I've half a mind to have a shot at him. just as a challenge."

"Or make him a signal," the doctor suggested. " 'Regret your baby overlaid during night.' "

"That would be tempting providence too far," Murrell told him. "But it is a pity we can't, because I'd like to twist his tail. We're not home yet."

"You're telling me," Macmillan said.

The Yeoman, with a pad in his hand, came to the two officers. Murrell, taking the signals, glanced at the top one. "The Commander-in-Chief compliments us on the way we take advantage of our opportunities," he told the doctor.

"Nice of him," Macmillan said. "You'd think we were doing this of our own choosing."

"We're all getting a lot more used to it. I'd hate to lose the old cow now. Yeoman — you can put a copy of that signal on the ship's notice board."

"There's another signal, sir," Willis said.

Murrell turned the lead. "Good heavens! *Northern Belle* and *Bromwich Town.*"

141

"What about them?" Macmillan asked.

"A couple of anti-submarine trawlers being sailed today as close escort. They should be with us about dawn tomorrow. *And* the salvage tug *Ocean Queen* sailing tomorrow. Things are happening at last!" Murrell paused and went on, "Queer thing — I'll be glad to see the trawlers. They were attached to the Fortieth Group when I commissioned the *Orchid* and when Wheeler was one of my two very raw sub-lieutenants. Yes, even if the officers have changed since I knew them, I'll be glad to see them again. But I'm not so sure about the tug. I said I'd hate to lose the cow; maybe I'd not feel like handing her over to anyone else either!"

"You will," the doctor said. "I bet you!"

For a moment, while both men thought, there was a silence. Murrell found, to his surprise, that he could again allow himself to think of Susan and Ginna and Peter in a way which had for the past three days been impossible. Men had their own methods of finding means to combat strain and anxiety. When matters were urgent, the mind found panacea in complete absorption in the business on hand. It was as if during the past days, the extent of life had been foreshortened to the foreseeable end of the job. Nothing mattered except its fulfilment. What lay beyond had become of minor importance. Now, at the easing of strain, the line of life had projected itself forward again to re-embrace that on which it had feared to lay its hopes. Wife, children and home, which for three days had been seen, if at all, through and behind a frosted glass of fear, were now seen clearly again. It was a pleasant sensation that went a long way to banish his awful fatigue and brought a smile to lips that were caked with a salt that tasted slightly of funnel gas.

The doctor was experiencing much the same sensation of re-entry into the future. His yacht, his hospital ward 142

and his many friends had all come into his life again. And although his eye for the *Antioch's* cavorting was as keen as ever, in his mind he saw a long sea loch that wound its sun-gilt waters between heather-covered mountains. He felt the gentle tug of the tiller within the palm of his hand, and the caress of the breeze in his ears, heard the softly intermittent swish of the bow wave as the yacht beat up against the light head wind; and as Macmillan filled and lit his pipe, it would have been impossible for him to say whether he stood duffel-coated and muffled on *Hecate's* bridge, or lolled in the sun-drenched cockpit of his own small *Thule*. Which was reality?

"What were we talking about?" Murrell, coming back with an effort from planning the completion of the concrete paddling pool, reopened the conversation with the doctor.

"Eh?" Macmillan asked.

"I said, what were we talking about?" Murrell explained patiently. "Because if it wasn't important, I have something that is."

"Such as what?" The doctor shuffled away into a drawer of the mind the thoughts of whether or no *Thule's* old mainsail would do for the first season after the war, and what the price of a new suit of sails would then be. "Such as what?" he repeated. He wondered why they both kept repeating phrases. Perhaps it was just their several tirednesses.

"Last night's effort has muddled up our watch-keeping," Murrell reminded him. "If you hand over to me now, I suggest you relieve me at ten. You'll take from ten until twelve thirty. If we split the forenoon, we'll be back in our usual watches."

127

"Suits me." Macmillan began to unfasten the telephone.

"Hear that?" the Captain asked sharply.

"What?" Macmillan paused in surprise.

"A man singing somewhere! It's the first song. I've heard since we took to tugging."

"Now you mention it, I do believe you're right," the doctor said. "Now that's a funny thing — fancy *my* not noticing something as important as that! I must be tired."

"You were too deeply committed yourself," Murrell suggested. "You'll not realize what the *Antioch* has done to us all until you're out of it."

"But we've still got her." Macmillan jerked a gloved hand in her direction.

"Maybe," Murrell said, "but not the U-boat!"

The Captain, before he took the telephone from the doctor's hands, glanced around the horizon. "That plane's going away!" he said, and, "I just wonder what he's going to tell his pals back home — and wouldn't I love to be in the Staff Office at Lorient when his report comes in!"

Masters brought the decoded weather chart.

"What's it like today?" Murrell asked as he took it in his gloved hands.

"Not so bad, sir," Masters replied. "At least from our point of view. The anticyclone over Europe is intensifying nicely, and creeping out into the Atlantic. It's already turned one depression to the south and may well do the same to the next."

Murrell beat his arms across his body. "It's brought some Russian cold with it. God, it's so cold the sea smells of caviar!"

"We may run into a belt of snow," Masters said.

"However much I hate the stuff, at least it will hide us," Murrell told them. "I feel dreadfully naked in this visibility — not that I think we're really in need of shelter. If prisoner Voss is right, they haven't another U-boat hereabouts, and we're too far out for their dive-bombers to interfere. They haven't enough Focke-Wulfs to risk. You don't really get reconnaissance 'jobs' being very offensive. If only the anticyclone will last for the next twenty-four hours, we'll be home before the tug arrives."

The doctor said, "Our friend the *Antioch* is towing rather nicely." And then, "You don't mention the cold?" Macmillan shivered.

"I didn't want to chill your enthusiasm."

"Enthusiasm?" Macmillan savoured the word. "I wonder if I still have any left?" He cocked his head to one side and answered his own question, "I think I have — I know I have."

"Well, she's all yours," Murrell said with gratitude as he took himself out of the cutting wind.

It was only ten minutes past eight when he reached his sea-cabin. Kirby had not yet brought up his breakfast. Still muffled, he stood by the radiator and looked out of the little scuttle. The most distant object he could see through the glass was the bulk of the *Antioch*. Seen through the hot haze that hung above the *Hecate's* funnels, her outline shimmered and shook: it became deliquescent and reminded him of scenes in films when someone is supposed to be drowning.

The object nearest to the scuttle was one of the stays of the foremast. It crossed the view diagonally and was little more than two feet away. Murrell watched a drop of water as, keeping to the lay of the wire rope, it spiralled downward. The drop stopped. Its stopping roused his greater interest and fixed his attention. It had no apparent reason to stop, and every reason why, with the help of the ship's vibration, it should have continued its journey. He moved closer to the scuttle and rubbed the glass. The crystal droplet had become opaque. It glowed like a pearl. He heard Kirby come into the cabin. "Was there any ice on the iron deck?" he asked without turning his head.

"Not on the deck yet, sir — but its forming on the stanchions and guardrails."

"I feared so." Murrell sat down to his meal.

"I'm afraid I slipped and lost your first breakfast — that's why I'm late, sir."

Murrell was becoming very tired, too tired even to express sympathy with his steward. He had to admit it. He was almost tempted to ask the doctor for a tablet of Benzedrine; but, after consideration, turned down the idea. He'd tried it once, and, although for a few hours he had been amazed at the vitality it brought him, he was sure that after the enlivening period was over he'd felt worse than if he'd never used the stuff. In an emergency it could be useful. In a convoy battle you could sometimes guess when the period of extreme effort would come and when it would end. With the *Antioch* you never knew, until it was too late, when things were going to happen.

This morning he really would break with routine and get his head down for a sleep. He thought he was too tired even to finish the meal that Kirby had brought. He did not want to offend Kirby. He went out into the cross-passage and opened the sliding door to the signal deck. There was no one in sight. He flung the food overboard. A hungry gull snatched it before it hit the water and flew away gulping. Murrell went back to his cabin and, in spite of the ten minutes it took for the soreness in his eyes to subside, he was asleep when his steward came again for the surreptitiously emptied plate.

## Chapter 18

Every morning after breakfast, von Fichte visited the Operations Room. Seeing the Admiral attended by his staff come down the passage, the sentry threw open the door. The Admiral, as he went in, was speaking over his shoulder to his Chief of Staff, and did not, in case he should have to recognize the presence of Herr Spichern, glance in the direction of the plot. But when he did look, he stopped short.

*"Herr Leutnant,"* he said to the young plotting officer, "what is that?" His finger pointed at the .yellow counter.

"The position of the tanker and destroyer as reported by Reconnaissance Wing at oh-seven-four-five this morning, Herr Admiral." All the faces of the staff were turned to the patch of bright yellow colour on the black table. The Admiral saw that Spichern was there, but with the plaque the centre of interest there was now no need to acknowledge his presence. No one spoke.

"Have you checked the report?" In silence the officer handed the Admiral a typewritten signal. It was shorter than usual. Reconnaissance had had a bad morning. They had sighted very little beyond the two ships which were the subject of the unhappy plaque. The Admiral glanced through it and dropped it on the table. "U-506? Has she reported?"

"Nothing, Herr Admiral."

"Did she not answer the nine o'clock routine call?"

"I do not think so, Herr Admiral. But I will check."

The Admiral glanced at his watch: "If she has not, have her called immediately — using the emergency prefix." The Lieutenant hurried from the room. Von Fichte waited, tapping his foot on the ground. No one had courage to break the silence. Five minutes passed. The officer returned. He looked scared.

"There is no reply — and she was called at the midnight 'optional' time too. She did not answer that either."

131

The Admiral stroked his heavy chin. Then he spoke slowly. "There are many things that could account for her silence. But I fear that by some miracle or other the British have scored another success. *Herr Kapitän,*" he turned to his Chief of Staff, "Have we no other boat near enough to intercept?"

"No, Herr Admiral."

"Then we must ask the Luftwaffe for help. Get me the Air Command Northwest. I'll take the call in my office."

"It's a long way for a medium bomber," the Chief of Staff suggested with deference.

The Admiral turned back to the plot.

Spichern unexpectedly said, "Yesterday, the Air General showed me six of the new long-range Heinkels. They'd only flown in the day before. He's very proud of them."

Von Fichte found himself unwilling to make use of this tool, but had no option. To do so made both the tool and the reason for its use infinitely more objectionable. It was only with the greatest difficulty that the Admiral managed, "Thank you, Herr Spichern. Your information comes at a most useful moment."

"I hope it will lead to success," Spichern said.

The eyes of journalist and Admiral met. "God in heaven!" the. Admiral exclaimed to himself, "the little bastard is threatening me!" Aloud, he repeated, "I'll take the call in my office." He turned away, and in turning tasted, for the first time for many years, the bitter forewarning of personal defeat if a project should go wrong. It must not go wrong.

But Air Command Northwest were not cooperatively minded. Hitler had too frequently changed the organization of the air-sea cooperation; and Admiral Doenitz was known to have quarrelled bitterly with *Reichsmarschall* Goering, the controller of the Luftwaffe. It was only natural that dissension at the summit should affect the work of those at lower levels.

The Air General wanted to know why the devil the U-boat arm could not do its own work? No. He had no long-range Heinkels. Well, yes. Perhaps that was not quite true. He had forgotten that he had shown them to that nasty little man the Navy had sent to him yesterday. No, no. He could not possibly send three — three was all that he had. Not on a wild goose chase that would take them halfway out into the Atlantic and back. Well, perhaps "halfway across the Atlantic" was an exaggeration — but four hundred miles from base was far enough in all conscience. He'd have the blood of that Spichern if ever he had the chance. Very well, he did have six Heinkels. But did not the Herr Admiral know that they had been sent to him specially to attack coastal shipping in the Bristol Channel and Irish Sea. No, he wouldn't! Well, only if Reconnaissance Wing would send out a recce plane to "home" his aircraft onto their target. If this could not be arranged, it was altogether too far at sea. Very well, three planes could be airborne at two in the afternoon — but only if Reconnaissance would cooperate. Otherwise U-boat Command could go to the devil and take their targets with them.

Wearily, the Admiral put down the telephone. "How they get made Air Generals defeats me," he muttered, and, raising the phone, demanded a connection to Reconnaissance Group 40, Bordeaux.

At Bordeaux they were primarily concerned with the Atlantic, and proved much more helpful.

Then he had to call Air Command Northwest again.

Shortly after noon the Chief of Staff reported to von Fichte that there had been no further word from U-506, and added: "But, Herr Admiral, the Monitoring Service have now turned in a belated report of a transmission at 22.48 last night. It was in cipher and they haven't been able to decode it, but the signal form suggests it was either a sighting report or else the report after a successful attack."

"I suppose," the Admiral said, as he looked with sombre eyes across the desk, "that you are only giving me the information in this indirect way because you know damn well that the signal *was* made by the destroyer. Or are you going to tell me that it came from a position which might have been ... when you know, and I know, that it was?"

The Staff Captain shrugged his shoulders. The Admiral went on, "And do you think I don't know that the use of cipher confirms our supposition? Sighting reports, *Herr Kapitän,* are *not* made in cipher. Of course we can't be certain. Lachmann's boat may only be damaged. But I think both you and I have already taken U-506 from the list of operational boats in the command. It is now imperative that for our eye — we have an eye *and* a tooth."

"The Heinkels should do that," the Staff Captain said.

The Admiral nodded. "Their senior officers may seem peculiar to our naval minds, but their airmen are good — and very well-trained. Flying low in formation, they will be very difficult to hit, and from that low height the bombs, when released, have a trajectory that is more like that of a shell. Unless they are shot down before they reach the point of bomb-release, they can't miss."

"No, Herr Admiral. I do not think they will miss." The Chief of Staff saluted and left the room.

## Chapter 19

In the *Hecate's* bridge the doctor was bitterly cold. The wind, which in the early morning had blown fitfully from all directions, had now settled down to a steady stream of air flowing out of the high-pressure system to the east of them. Originating in a Russian winter, it had lost nothing of its cruel bite in its passage across the North Sea: it stung the eyes, froze the fingers and, creeping beneath the buttoned oilskins or duffel-coats, invaded the privacy of human bodies. It was a drying wind: it cracked men's lips and made their eyes sore; it dried out the wooden plinth on which the compass stood, until it looked as if it had just been holystoned; it drew the moisture out of everything that had been wet. The signal halyards, like the boughs of a winter tree, crackled and whispered as they were agitated by the wind, and tiny crystals of salt formed on the bridge windscreens where the spray was dried to brine.

Steaming straight into the wind's eye, the ship was remarkably steady. She pitched only very slightly, and when she rolled, she did so with a quick jerky motion which was no more than a shrug of her shoulders. The tow rope led straight to the bluff-bowed *Antioch,* following dutifully in her wake. The sky to the north and east darkened until, as it reached over them, it was like the mouth of a great cave — a cave into whose recess they steamed, awe-inspired and solemn. The illusion of something both solid and startling stretching above them was made more intense by the horizon, which, as sharp-edged as the lip of a silver bowl, was shot with a livid sheen.

"We'll be as easily seen as specks on a mirror," Macmillan observed to Masters, who happened to pass him. He felt conspicuously naked, with the sensation that unseen eyes mocked his shame. "Babes in the Wood," he said, "that's what we are. Just babes in the bloody wood. My God, it's cold!"

"It's going to snow," Masters said. "It may be warmer when it does."

"It'll cut visibility to nearly nothing. How are we going to tow then?"

"It will be here soon. There's the edge of it, not more than a couple of miles away. Do you think we ought to call the Captain?"

" 'Deed and I don't know," the doctor said. "He's so tired I'd rather let him sleep — speaking as a doctor."

"But it *is* his responsibility," Masters reminded him.

Macmillan looked unhappy; he rubbed his cold pipe on his cold nose and left a coal-black smear. He saw that the Navigator wanted the Captain to be called because then he, Masters, would feel safer. Come to think of it, he too would like to feel the Captain's authority by his side. Perhaps he, the professional man, had always considered Murrell the junior partner in their friendship. Now he wanted him badly. "I suppose so," he said.

"I'll go and call him." Masters, having obtained agreement, was in a hurry.

Murrell thought that the fog in his brain solidified and filled his mouth. It stuck to his tongue, and yet he knew it had to be swallowed if consciousness were to be regained. It was a sensation of near-panic. He rolled angrily on his bunk and his throat worked in time with the noise in his ears. Then the cotton-wool had gone and he was left leaning on one arm with his throat sore. The knocking on his door was repeated. The knuckles struck the woodwork with urgency. "Come in," he croaked.

"There's a snowstorm coming up," Masters told him.

"Snow?" Murrell whispered. "Snow? So what the hell?"

"We won't be able to see the tow from the bridge, sir. The doctor and I, we thought we'd better call you."

"Of course," Murrell said. "Of course. I'm sorry if I was slow to understand." He struggled to a sitting position and slid his trousered legs over the bunk's side.

Masters felt it kinder to leave Murrell to perform his recovery from sleep alone. He thought the Captain looked tired and far from well. He was glad that he had taken the message himself — and not sent a sailor.

"I'll be up in a minute," Murrell called after the Navigator. "Tell the doctor not to worry."

He was always telling people "not to worry." Always doing the worrying himself. He stood up and dragged the duffel-coat over his arms.

At first only a few feathery flakes came wistfully down, and then, all at once, the storm was on them. Drifting like the dead leaves of autumn, the flakes fell slantwise and in continuously observable succession into the sea, which swallowed them up as if they had never been. But where the wind that bore them was deflected in its passage over the ship, the eddying air stream carried the snowflakes all ways. Often defying gravity, they were flung aloft, and so appeared to cross and crisscross their fellows going down to the waves.

The flakes mantled the ships with white and picked out, with the hand of an artist, a line here or a curve there. They settled on gun barrels and blew along the deck to pile comfortably into little triangular drifts in odd corners. Then, when anyone went up a ladder, they would take off from their resting place and fly icily about his face. On the bridge they drifted with satanic glee into corners where no storm had ever carried water. The chart in the charthouse was reduced to pulp, and the Yeoman to fury when he found his spare pads were soaked. Unbelievably lovely the *Hecate* may have looked, but she could not see herself, nor could her Captain see the *Antioch*.

So the snow brought a new problem. The stern of their ship was six hundred feet from the bow of the tow. Their own bridge was a further two hundred feet away. This last, they discovered, made all the difference between seeing the *Antioch* dimly and not seeing her at all. Murrell and the doctor had to make a hurried journey to the stern of the destroyer and do their tug-mastering from the open shelter behind the after house.

A telephone led from there to the bridge and helm, and speed orders could be easily passed to the Officer of the Watch. But the change of position produced a problem. For the last four days they had trained themselves, as much by instinct as by thought, to counteract the swing and adjust the pull that one ship had on the other. To do this, they had taught their eye to use the two-hundred-foot-long sighting bar of their own ship, and to judge by the way she swung what orders they should give to counteract the pull.

But now that they stood aft, directly above the propellers and the rudder which they were trying to control, they had lost their sighting bar. What they had learned to achieve with comparative ease from the bridge was much more difficult from their new position. The "tug-masters" were both desperately tired. The snow sometimes fell refreshingly on taut-skinned faces; at other times it drifted into sore eyes, crept irritatingly down their necks, and even allowed itself to be drawn into their nostrils.

The Captain and doctor ate their lunch standing up in the corner of the shelter. The two had been together since eleven o'clock, experimenting with ways to manage the tow: an interest so absorbing that they had come to consider the art of towing as the main part of their enterprise. It was as a disturbance that they regarded the signalman who came paddling along the snow-covered deck. The Captain read the signal aloud.

"C-in-C Western Approaches to *Hecate*. Trawlers and *Ocean Queen* sailing from Londonderry 10.00 today. *Hecate* is to signal rendezvous to ships concerned."

The Captain tapped the thin paper with his gloved finger. "You'll observe, Doc, that there's a catch in it."

"Meaning?" Macmillan queried.

"That if they are sailing from Londonderry at ten o'clock this morning they are going to meet with us about dusk tonight; that there's a hell of a tide runs backwards and forwards along the north coast of Ireland; that, as we're going, we'll pick up the tide off Bloody Foreland with two hours to spare and carry it all the way to Rathlin Island; that if, for some reason, we miss that flood tide, we'll make no progress over the land for damn nigh six hours; that it may well take an ocean tug all of that time to get rid of the lash-up that we are towing with and get her own men and wires aboard; that the tug won't try doing so in the dark. In fact, my friend, any alteration to present circumstances that delays us more than two hours is going to mean that the *Antioch* will be another day at sea."

"She's floating well enough," the doctor remarked.

"She may be at the moment," Murrell answered, "but don't forget the enemy. I bet there's a very angry Admiral in Lorient. An angry man will try all sorts of things you don't expect." The Captain put down his cup of coffee and patted his stomach. "I only hope the Herr Admiral has enjoyed his lunch as much as I have," he said, and then, his thought returning to its earlier train: "And those tugs have only lieutenants in command."

"Meaning that the tug's captain will be junior to you?"

"So long as we are left with the party," Murrell agreed. "If it had been three, or even two days ago we'd have been given a definite order that would have released us for home as soon as the tug had arrived. But now, when the Staff ashore will think us so nearly there, they'll assume we'll be only too ready to slip off and they won't make any signal at all."

"Then the decision, when it has to be made, will be entirely ours?" Macmillan asked.

"Entirely mine." Murrell made the small correction, and the doctor, watching his captain closely, could find no arrogance in the remark at all.

## *Chapter 20*

It's not just a question of who last had sleep," Macmillan said to the Captain. "Although even there I'm really better off than you. To be woken up after little more than an hour — as this morning you were — is more likely to reduce your efficiency than having no sleep at all. I'm not telling you for the good of your own health — it's the ship that needs you."

"But it *is* your turn to sleep," Murrell said defiantly, and added, "Who's captain here?"

"I don't care what you are. If you won't take my advice as a friend, I'll bloody well start throwing my medical weight around."

"I can tell you to go to hell!"

"Oh, no you can't," the doctor said. "Almost anyone else on earth while they are on your ship — but not the ship's doctor. I've not been in the Navy long enough to know the ins and outs of all the regulations — but I can tell you this — that a determined medico can do more or less just what he likes and get away with it. You could, of course, have me court-martialled afterwards, and I'd have to answer for anything I'd done. It could be quite a *cause célèbre*. Shall we try — I'm game."

"I'm not your patient!"

"Not yet — but you will be. Now for heaven's sake, go along and get your head down."

And Murrell, who was really too exhausted for argument, allowed himself to be persuaded.

At two o'clock, as the anticyclone pushed further out into the Atlantic and the *Hecate* crawled slowly homeward, they ran out of the snow as suddenly as they had entered it.

In the pale sunshine of a winter's afternoon the ships looked unreal and insubstantial. Delicately fragile, they seemed to be made of ice: ice that might dissolve and disappear, melting into the sea that carried them. Seeing them so ethereal, the doctor, halfway through his watch and tired beyond belief, felt himself a phantom man.

With the passing of the snow Macmillan left the after house and went back to the bridge. Gray was on watch and Masters about the bridge. The Navigator went to speak to the doctor. He brought with him a cup of cocoa. Referring to the ships he said, "They look like a couple of ghosts — makes you wonder if you're already dead. Even the men changed watch without talking. The cold freezes thought. Did you notice that at the change of the watch no one spoke. Men saw their relief arrive, heads nodded, eyes flickered and the change-over was made."

The doctor sipped his drink. "Even if it does burn your lips — this kai's good." He put down his cup on the top of a flag locker. For once he had no wish to encourage his companion's flights of fancy.

Masters said, "How's our child behaving? You know, I really can't begin to imagine life without her. I'd feel quite lonely!"

"She's doing very well. She seems to like this head wind. Now that the westerly swell is almost dead, and she's only got these short seas from ahead to meet, she's really giving very little trouble."

A signalman came out on the bridge. He had a worried look, and his eyes glanced forward to the compass platform where Gray, the gunner, stood, and then aft to where the doctor talked to Masters. Masters was a lieutenant and a ship's officer, and as far as the signalman was concerned, the doctor was not a ship's officer. Guessing the cause of the indecision, Masters called to him, "I'll take it." The man brought him the paper. Together doctor and Navigator read the message which was prefixed "most immediate." It read: "Enemy aircraft are being 'homed' onto you. You should anticipate air attack between now and sunset."

When they had read the message the two officers looked away. The sun was already sinking into the sunset blush of easterly weather. Like a colony of bats before sunset the frost in the signal halyards chirruped and cheeped. The horizon, as the sun set, was iron-hard. Since the snow, the sea had been the green of old jade; but as the sun sank a few degrees, it became gray — except when the low light shone momentarily through a wavetop to turn the translucent pinnacle to the green of new grass.

"I think I'd better take it down to him," Masters said, remembering the morning.

"It seems a pity. I suppose we can't just go to action stations and hope he doesn't wake up?" the doctor suggested.

"It wouldn't be fair to him, Doc. Supposing they were to come in so quickly that he didn't have time to get on the bridge?"

"You're right," Macmillan sighed. "You'd better tell him."


Masters shook his captain's arm — then his shoulder. "Captain, sir. Captain." Murrell's head turned as his body was moved, but his breathing remained deep and regular.

"Captain, sir, Captain!" Masters was frankly bewildered. He had not previously met the druglike sleep of utter exhaustion and found the experience as unnerving as if he had come across his captain's dead body. "Please, sir." But there was no answer. And then quite suddenly Murrell sat up. His eyes opened.

"Signal from Admiralty. Most immediate. Enemy aircraft are being 'homed' onto you. You should anticipate air attack between now and sunset." Masters, holding the message for Murrell to read, was just a little surprised that the Captain neither read it for himself nor showed any emotion.

But Murrell's next words satisfied him. "Go to action stations at once. Pass that signal to *Antioch* for information and tell Wheeler to man his guns. I'll be up directly."

Masters hurried from the cabin. He was not too old to anticipate the thrill of pressing the alarm button himself: of the chance to trigger off the chain reaction that would turn the destroyer into a fighting weapon.

Murrell sat on in his bunk. Slowly his head fell forward. His shoulders sagged. He went on sleeping because he had never woken up. It was his subconscious mind that had answered Masters' call with the correct solution. The *Hecate's* Captain did not even hear the racket of his ship preparing for action. He slept.

With the sinking of the U-boat, the men of the *Antioch* had experienced the same lightening of tension that had refreshed the Hecates. And, because they were afloat in what was the main target, their sense of relief was even more intense.

On that morning Wheeler, tentatively opening the picture album of memory, found that, whereas on previous occasions since he had been in the *Antioch* the book could only be glanced at and then immediately shut, it could now be left open and studied with care and attention. He was now quite certain that he was going to marry Anne.

Conditions of life in the wheelhouse were improving. Hart, using fire clay and firebricks that had been found in the ship's stores, had made a very serviceable stove, using for the chimney a piece of circular ventilating trunk with an angled bend that he had been able to tear down from the empty cabins. The bend, when the pipe had been fixed, allowed the chimney to pass out of the wheelhouse through a hole cut in one of the wooden shutters. And as a precaution against sparks — they had only wood to burn — a bucket had been made into a cowl.

The difference that this had made to life in the wheelhouse was out of all proportion to the slight damage that had been done to the ship, and as the men kept their watch just beside the makeshift funnel it was easy for them to see that the fire was low enough to prevent sparks.

Although the situation of the men in the *Antioch* was distinctly less pleasant than it was for the Hecates, they had physically had nothing like so arduous a time. The destroyer had been forced to turn out both watches each time that she had recovered the tow, and in addition to the normal work of the ship they had had to launch the decoy and fight an action with the enemy. The *Antioch's* men were not short of sleep, and Wheeler had no idea of the tiredness that overwhelmed Murrell. To Wheeler, the destroyer was identified with her captain. He had watched her manoeuvre with precision and seen her attack with daring. It never occurred to him that her captain might have less strength than the steel of his ship.

143

In the afternoon Wheeler was reading a book that he had found aboard. His back was propped against pillows and his legs were thrust out along his mattress. White was on watch. Sibson and Anders were playing draughts, while Pengelley cleaned and filled the oil lamps ready for the night. The air was cosily warm, and, if the place was over-full of tobacco smoke, at least it had acquired the lived-in aspect of a home.

The sun, sinking into the west, no longer flooded the wheelhouse. Its rays only just tipped the starboard scuttles. Pengelley, bearing a lamp in his hand whose wick he was adjusting, moved across to the starboard side to catch the better light. Sibson lay on his belly with his face close against the draughtboard. To reach the light Pengelley had to pass close to his outstretched feet.

"Huff you!" Wheeler heard Anders' happy remark followed by the slap-slap as the draughtsmen were moved on the board.

Into this scene White burst through the door. "What the hell is it, man?" Wheeler asked.

"Signal, sir. Most immediate: we're to expect air attack between now and sunset. Another from *Hecate,* sir: you're to man the guns aboard here."

The news was a tight band of strain drawn around every head of those who heard it. Pengelley, stepping back, trod on the draughtboard.

"You silly Cornish bastard," Sibson said, "can't you control those flipping feet of yours?"

Pengelley said, "Don't you call me names you big lump ..."

Sibson sprang to his feet.

Wheeler shouted, "Be careful there, Pengelley."

Pengelley moved, his eyes watching Sibson had no care for his feet. He stumbled over Anders and fell. The lamp, shooting from his hand, spread paraffin oil across the floor. Eagerly the flame from their homemade stove leaped along the river of oil that ran to its door. Frantically the four men tried to beat it out; and then, when that was obviously impossible, for already the mattresses were burning fiercely, they ran for the fire extinguishers on the main deck, and brought them to the wheelhouse.

But with no heat on the ship these particular extinguishers had frozen. They were useless.

"Water. Water. Water!" Wheeler found himself calling desperately. Smoke, hot and acrid; swirled around him. He wanted to run but couldn't. A figure lurched out of the murk.

"What the hell d'ye think you are — a flipping duck?" it said, and would have hurried on. But Wheeler laid hands on it. It was Sibson. It was obvious to the officer that the man was no longer a naval rating. He was just a very frightened man.

"You'll stop here!" Wheeler ordered.

"The hell I will! I ain't frying tonight for you nor nobody else." With a vicious wrench Sibson tore himself free, and was gone.

There was nothing Wheeler could do but let him go. There didn't appear much that Wheeler could do about the fire — or about anything else. There just wouldn't be time.

## Chapter 21

Like a needle sinking through anaesthetized flesh into the quick beyond, the shaking sank through Murrell's brain until at last a wakeful nerve was reached. "Captain, sir, Captain, sir. You wouldn't answer the phone."

"What is it, man?" Murrell gasped, swinging cramped limbs upright.

"Tow's on fire, sir!"

The Captain was out of the cabin as fast as he had ever been. Fourteen thousand tons of high-octane spirit was something to go on fire!

He had to push past men whom he was surprised to find already at their action stations. Seeing their captain, they tried instantly to get out of his way, but could not always do so. Breathless and battered, he reached the back of the bridge.

He found the ship heeled as she tugged at the tow, dragging the tanker around so that she would be beam-on to the wind. Thank God for the doctor! He had appreciated the position and acted.

Black billows of smoke rose from the burning wheelhouse, but he could see at a glance that, desperate as the situation might appear, it was not yet catastrophic. A signal lamp flickered from the starboard wing of the tanker's bridge as her bows were dragged around to the north.

"What is it, Yeoman?" Murrell called, as he leaped to the compass platform.

"Fire extinguishers useless. Can you supply?" the Yeoman told him the signal.

"Reply 'Yes, will come alongside your starboard quarter to put fire party aboard.' "

To Gray, "Slip the tow."

To the wheelhouse, "Pipe the fire party to muster on the fo'c'sle with all the extinguishers from the ready-use stowage."

To the quartermaster, "Starboard fifteen. One-eight-oh revolutions."

To Gray, "Thank you, Gray — I'll take her. Will you lead the fire party. You'll have to jump for it — but it won't be too bad."

To Thompson, "Go down and collect enough men to hang every fender you can find round the port bow."

The *Hecate,* describing a half-circle, swept around to windward of the tanker. As her bow edged toward the rolling ship, Murrell set the doctor, who was the only officer left on the bridge, at the voice pipe and himself leaped to the port wing of the bridge. "Repeat my orders, Doctor. Slow both."

As the destroyer crept toward the tanker, the ships appeared to roll more and more heavily. It was only the proximity to another vessel that gave the illusion. Murrell realized then that considerable damage would be done to his own ship, but now that he had embarked on the proceeding, there was no other way.

Already below him the ship's side had been festooned with fenders, their rope lanyards tied to the guardrails. The boarding party, sixteen strong, waited. Half of the men carried the scarlet cylinders of the extinguishers and half the buckets that each held four refills. And two white-helmeted engine-room ratings held asbestos suits over their arms, ready to put them on as soon as they had made the jump.

As the distance between the ships closed, Murrell saw that he had chosen wisely in deciding to go alongside the stern. The after deck of the tanker was only some three feet higher than his own bows, and, as the ships rose and fell in the sea, there would be a time when the decks would be level. "Starboard ten. Stop port. Half astern starboard."

The *Hecate* vibrated gently. The distance narrowed until it could be measured in feet. The burning wheelhouse could no longer be seen. It was hidden by the funnels and the fore part of the after superstructure. There were only the heavy billows of black smoke.

"Stand by to jump when you have a chance," Murrell shouted.

"Stop both."

The *Hecate's* shoulders nudged the tanker. Two men leaped. The ships rolled apart and together again — but this time much more heavily. Torn metal screamed and there was the heavy crunch of bent guardrails. More men went across. Like a man amputating his own damaged limb, Murrell watched the quarter-inch plating of his light ship pounded against the heavier hull. Blood-red streaks on the tanker's side showed where paint had been rubbed off. And there were dents too.

"Half astern together. Port fifteen," the Captain ordered. The destroyer, shaken by battering her shoulder against the tanker, vibrated to the power of her own engines. She gave one more nudge that was almost friendly, and then drew away. Murrell took her back again toward the burning ship — but a cable clear to windward so that they could see what went on. Already they had seen the men of the fire party clambering up the double ladders. Men in dungarees, and men in yellow duffel-coats, men in blue serge trousers and jerseys, just as they had had the call; but all having one thing in common — a scarlet canister under their arms or a scarlet bucket swinging from a handle. The bright-red blobs scampered like ants up the ladders, and were followed by two more slowly moving men in white asbestos clothing. They too disappeared towards the high bridge of the tanker.

The Captain, in the first free moment since he had rushed from his cabin, turned to the doctor. "Doc," he said, "how is it that the men are at action stations? Who sent them there?"

Macmillan with surprise said, "You did."

"No," Murrell said. "No! When?"

"When Masters took the signal about the aircraft to you."

"What aircraft? What do you mean!" Murrell clutched his friend's arm. The world was not so much mad, as unhinged.

Macmillan saw the look of dismay that could turn to fear. He said, "Don't let it worry you. It often happens in cases of exhaustion. Men act correctly but don't know what they do."

"Get me the signal," Murrell demanded.

Macmillan, going to fetch the signal pad from the chart house, said gently, "You put up a damn fine show going alongside that tanker — you're all right."

"Damn your bedside manner." Murrell spoke with sharp cruelty. "Whatever you may say, it feels horrid. Will you get me the signal!"

It was the nearest to a snap that he had ever made at the doctor. He felt ashamed of himself, but took a vicarious pleasure in the shame. As if by his being beastly he justified his captaincy. His mouth was cloyed with the sweet taste of extreme weariness, and around his head was a tourniquet of fatigue: its pressure greatest on a spot behind and above his left ear. He took off his cap for relief — but found none. Only the cold wind snapped at his bared scalp to cause discomfort without refreshment. He replaced his cap and looked again at the *Antioch*.

The heavy smoke blowing to leeward and pressed flat to the sea by the cold wind made the ship look as if she had developed a list to port. But after a moment's acute anxiety, Murrell satisfied himself that this was an optical illusion. The smoke pall, growing in height as it blew clear of the big ship, made her appear to have canted. If, deep within himself, he had fear for the lives of the twenty men he had put aboard her, he neither showed nor allowed himself to feel it. He was riding himself hard: riding down imagination, cutting at consideration for other lives. If matters went right, all would be well. If they went wrong and the *Antioch* blew up, it would be a burden of guilt to carry for the rest of his days.

Macmillan brought him the pad. There was the signal from the Admiralty and the one that had been made to the *Antioch*. "I suppose I sent this signal too?" he asked.

Macmillan nodded.

Murrell tore his mind from the personal problem. It would have to wait. He went to the voice pipe that led to the Radar Office. "Can you find any aircraft?"

"No, sir. We've had a small echo from time to time, but only for a second or two."

"If it stays up in the cloud layer, I suppose we're unlikely to pick it up?" Murrell asked.

"That's it, sir. If it stays behind the clouds we shan't have much chance of finding it with this 'surface to surface' set."

"And anyway it will stay out of range," Murrell said to the doctor. "These 'homers' are very careful of themselves."

"The bloody swine. After all we've done!"

"Not on your life — that fellow up there is a godsend: worth his weight in gold! If he wasn't chattering to his pals, we'd never know they were coming!"

The Engineer Officer came on the bridge to report the extent of the damage. "Well, Chief, what have I done?" Murrell asked.

"The heads and bathrooms, sir. Smashed in the carline and broken the water pipes. I've had to disconnect the lot, sir.

"Good Lord, what a place to smash up — buckets — how horrid."

"Can't be helped, sir — and it won't be so bad, so long as we can get the bastard in."

"Do you really mean when 'we get her in,' or are we going to hand over to the tug when she comes?" Murrell asked. He was interested to learn what another thought.

"I don't reckon that *Antioch* would be safe with only a tug to look after her, sir. Never known such a ship for trouble!"

"What about your stokers?"

"They're all right, sir. Of course it was a little difficult for them to start with — all those alterations of speed. It wasn't easy, and, as you know, we couldn't help but make smoke sometimes."

Looking again at the *Antioch,* Murrell saw that the character of the smoke had changed. The sunset tinge of flame seemed to be less, and the black smoke from the burning paint-layered wood was mixed around its base with the light-gray haze from the chemical extinguishers. To the doctor he said, "There's just a chance the gamble may come off — I could wish the stakes were less. One doesn't like to think of the men.... It's difficult to decide whether I have sent them there because the nation needs the tanker home — or just because I'm determined to get her in."

"You can't think of things in that light," Macmillan said.

"What else can you do but think? It isn't as though I personally had anything to do. I'm just standing here — waiting."

"Aircraft green eight-oh." The cry came from the starboard side. "See 'em — low on the water. Three of them."

The German planes were coming in with the advantage of the darkening night behind them, and they had the ships in silhouette against the arc of lighter sky. They were so close to the sea that they only just cleared the waves.

"Heinkels!" the Captain exclaimed as he dived for the compass platform. "How the hell do they get Heinkels out here! Range ten thousand. Rapid independent. Shoot. Port ten. Steer oh-four-five."

The two long 4.7 guns began to fire. Boom — boom — boom. The *Hecate* started to move out diagonally to Murrell to bring an enfilading fire on anything attacking his charge.

"Range seven thousand." Looking at the enemy the Captain said grimly, "Obviously the first team. I'm afraid they mean real business. We've stirred up a hornets' nest."

With the reduced range, the shell bursts from the guns were nearer. The shooting was good, but it was terribly difficult to hit the low black planes against the dark backdrop of eastern cloud. The aircraft were in reverse arrowhead formation. Each of the leaders was aiming for a ship. The third was potentially the most dangerous, for there was a chance that he would succeed in making his attack without ever being fired at. The Bofors gun in the stern of the tanker opened up. Chump — chump — chump. It had a curiously satisfying sound — like someone chopping wood in a garden.

"Mr. Thompson," the Captain said, "shift fire of main armament to the third plane, as soon as the close-range weapons can engage the first two."

A second later a terrific clatter sounded on the bridge as the single-barrelled port bridge. Oerlikon and the double-barrelled midship Oerlikons opened up together. Satisfying streams of red tracer bullets soared confidently toward the planes. *Antioch's* two Oerlikons on the port side were firing.

"Range five thousand."

Boom — boom; chump — chump — chump; and the continual racket of the Oerlikons. At close range Murrell couldn't do anything more. It was up to the individual gunlayers. Whatever the outcome, the enemy had — thanks to the warning signal — been given a reception.

151

## Chapter 22

For a moment, after Sibson's sudden disappearance, Wheeler had been alone in the throat-catching smoke; the next he found himself in clean air, with the pillows of smoke blown to leeward. With intense and heartened relief he realized the *Hecate's* part in this as he saw her struggling to pull the tanker around beam to the wind. Others were trying to save the ship, and that helped a lot.

There were some of his own men about too. He recognized the signalman. "White," he called. "Make a signal to *Hecate*. Tell them our fire extinguishers are useless. Ask if they can supply." He had no idea how this was to be done. It was little more than a cry for help that carried an explanation of their difficulties. At the same time it had something of the blind faith of a child — that something would be done. With one wing of the burning bridge clear, White would be able to use his lamp. The destroyer was on that side of the *Antioch* and could read it.

Hart staggered toward him coughing, and Pengelley followed. Trotman and Anders joined them as the smoke cleared and they could see. In their extremity they looked to Wheeler as he looked to Murrell.

"If we aren't a flipping beacon for flipping aircraft, I don't know what is." Trotman spoke both in wonder and awe.

Hart said, "Where's that Sibson?"

"He's gone," Wheeler told them.

"Gorn? How? When?" They all spoke together.

Wheeler wanted to laugh. The situation had more than a touch of farce. Five of them talking on the deck of a blazing oil well, White happily tapping his lamp; and because death was so near, they had misunderstood his use of the word "gone."

"I didn't mean he's dead. He's just run away. God knows where he is now!"

"Pity," Hart said. "He's our torpedoman. He ought to know about electrics. Fire runs down the cables, that I do know. Oughtn't we to cut them off close to the deckhead? If we could keep it to this deck, it might burn itself out."

"Excellent," Wheeler said. "Take the others with you and patrol the cabins below. Do everything you can to prevent the fire spreading there. Cut all the cables you can find. Watch out for smouldering cork and paint dropping from above."

White came with the message from Murrell, "Will come alongside your starboard quarter to put fire party aboard." Wheeler read it aloud to his little group of unshaven men. It was as if Murrell himself had arrived among them: Murrell dressed in his best uniform, ready to go ashore on some sunlit quay and acting a little the part of The Destroyer Captain.

"Puts heart into you, don't it?" Pengelley expressed the relief of all.

"Come on," Wheeler said, free now that he had had the reply to his signal. He led the way down the ladder to the deck below. The others followed. Before the door there was a moment of hesitation. All were conscious of the petrol beneath their feet. Although being inside would make no difference to the speed of their death, it was nicer to be on deck. Wheeler opened the door. A waft of hot air laced with the smell of scorched paint rushed out to meet them. "We're not too soon!" Wheeler said. "Come on, chaps!" He ran in.

Already, smouldering paint was peeling from the deck above. In the choking atmosphere they moved from cabin to cabin, beating, stamping at the fallen fragments. Hart, a handkerchief bound over his nose, was trying to cut and pull down the electric cables. All the time the atmosphere was getting worse, the heat greater. They discarded duffel-coats, flung off their sweaters. Perspiration poured down their bodies, and their eyes ran with the smoke. The pain in their eyelids made more tears run. These cut wavering avenues through the grime.

They staggered from cabin to cabin, going ever more slowly. A carpet burst into flames. It was a blaze beyond the control of stamping feet. The smoke from it was heavy, driving them back, forcing them toward the open door. "Christ! It ain't no use," Hart said. "If this deck goes alight, she's a goner. I reckon it's time to look after ourselves!"

"No," Wheeler said, "not yet. Perhaps the heat will have melted the ice in the extinguishers. There're two in this alley way. You take the one by the door — I'll go for the one at the other end." He disappeared, coughing, into the smoke and holding his hand over his mouth.

"He's a bloody fool," Trotman said as they waited. "Come on, let's go." But as he spoke they heard the hissing noise of water atomized under great pressure. Momentarily the smoke was lulled and Wheeler's figure was seen tensed in a doorway. He held the conical extinguisher like a lance in rest. He came back to the group. "Carpet's out," he gasped.

Hart shook his head. "Maybe so, sir. But it's got beyond us."

Wheeler saw that no one had made a move to get the other extinguisher. The men had convinced themselves of the hopelessness of the endeavour. They wouldn't go back, and Wheeler couldn't blame them. One by one they slipped out of the open door and hurried down the ladder to the main deck below. Wheeler went to the door for air. He wondered what he should do now. When his crew had gone, there didn't seem much that he could do alone. He watched his men as they ran aft along the deck, and then saw the slim bow of the destroyer move alongside.

Then there were many men — there seemed to be far more than the eighteen — running toward him along the deck. The newcomers met and swept up his own retreating men, carrying them back with the momentum of their own scurrying, purposeful feet. They came fresh with energy and carried in their hands the canisters of saving chemical. Leading them, Gray charged up the ladder. "Hello, Number One," he said. "Hadn't you better get some clothes on? You'll catch your death!" He ran past the astonished Wheeler up to the deck above.

For the rest of his life Wheeler was to wonder where personal fear went for the next ten minutes. And the only conclusion he could ever draw was that when faced with the inevitable man could ignore the obvious, completely closing one part of his mind to one particular probability — that of the imminent explosion beneath his feet.

Rather shamefacedly his own crew, worsted in their fight with the flames, gathered around their officer. They neither spoke nor moved. The eyes of all but White watched the men trained as firemen, who for the first time had the chance to put their training into practice. But White, the signalman, kept his eyes outboard.

It was White who first drew attention to the three tiny dots.

"Man the guns," Wheeler cried, and oddly found the advancing enemy far more frightening than the threat of fire. In a moment his men had disappeared to become a crew again. With White, he ran up the ladder to the starboard bridge Oerlikon.

The *Hecate's* guns were firing. The shell bursts showed white against the black cloud. Then the destroyer's close-range weapons were firing, and White, beside him, was firing too.

Wheeler saw that the enemy were intent on pressing home their attack, and he too realized the danger of the third and last plane as specifically as Murrell had done. He moved over to stand beside White, intending, when the first plane had made its attack, to direct the signalman's fire to the last of the three.

The *Antioch's* Bofors and Oerlikons were engaging the left-hand plane, the *Hecate's* Oerlikons the right-hand one, while the destroyer's long-range armament was firing at the third. The planes were surrounded by the red dots of tracer that climbed like scarlet mice toward their targets — planes that seemed indestructible. And then the Bofors fell silent. Wheeler wondered if he should run aft to sec if he could help to clear the jam. But Pengelley knew more about the gun than he did himself, and in any case the attack would be over long before he had run even as far as the after superstructure.

Suddenly he realized that Sibson had been given the starboard gun beside the funnel — and God alone knew where Sibson was. Then White's gun jammed, leaving the ship momentarily defenceless. When he had helped to clear the bent cartridge that had caused the trouble, the leading plane was so close that he set White to fire at the last attacker.

But miraculously the gun by the funnel had begun to fire. For half a vital minute it was the *Antioch's* only defence.

The weapon was hidden from Wheeler's sight and he had no idea who fired it. All he could see was the lean black barrel that pulsed steadily as shell after shell left its muzzle.

The Heinkel was firing back with its cannon. Spurts of flame rippled along the leading edge of the wing, and the plane's nose was directed full at the gun.

Wheeler could see the shells bursting all around, but still the Oerlikon went on firing — and hitting. To Wheeler it had become a duel between the single gun and the massed cannon of the enemy, and time was inexplicably slowed. He could see the Oerlikon's tracer rip into the shiny black plane. It was terribly close now — and the Oerlikon had stopped. But so too had the guns of the Heinkel. For a hushed second there was silence — then one last, and very deliberate, shot came from the gun. Wheeler saw it smash through the perspex nose. The enemy plane tipped up sharply. Its whole pale-green underside was visible. But it wasn't going straight any more. It went upwards and sideways — over the ship. Its wing missed the funnel by a foot — no more. With a great splash it fell into the sea beyond. Then there was time to look around. White was still firing at the last plane, and he could hear again the happy chump — chump of the Bofors from behind the funnel. In front of the destroyer's bows there was a large oily patch with a black object sinking there — like a shark's fin when the fish dives.

The last Heinkel was turning. It was still half a mile away, but had broken off the attack. It did not look well, and, like a wild duck that has been wounded, it fluttered unhappily over the sea. Its head was around to the east. The destroyer was turning under full helm to keep her guns bearing. Wheeler thought that now that the plane was out of range of their gun he need not bother further about the enemy, and he stopped White from firing. Then he ran down the ladder and along the iron deck of the tanker to the gun by the funnel.

As he tore along the deck he caught sight of Hart also running from his side of the superstructure to the other. There were two flights of ladders to the boat deck. Wheeler pounded up them both, his footfalls echoing weirdly in the quiet of the deserted ship.

Hurrying around the windshield, which in peacetime had provided a sheltered corner for the engine-room officers, he came to the gun. The muzzle pointed upwards, while all around the wood of the deck and the metal side of the funnel base had been pock-marked by cannon shells. In the harness that was fastened to the breech hung what was left of Sibson. He was quite dead, for no man could take such injury and live. Hart turned as Wheeler joined him. He had, Wheeler saw, a look of wonder in his eyes, and the cold wind played with the slightly grizzled curls of his head. Wheeler too, rather self-consciously, took off his cap.

The two men looked at each other. "He fired last," Wheeler said.

"Yes, sir. He'd copped all this before he fired that last one."

Together they were silent, swaying slightly to the scend of the ship beneath their feet.

"Mr. Wheeler, sir. Mr. Wheeler." The distant voice hailed.

"Wait a minute, Hart." Wheeler went to the rail that looked over the deck to the bridge sixty feet away. White was hailing. His hands cupped his mouth and the words were long drawn out. "Signal ... from ... *Hecate*. Stand ... by ... to ... recover ... tow."

Wheeler waved his arm to show that he had heard. Then he went back. Hart had clipped the gun in its housed position. And over a heap that lay behind it he was drawing a winch cover. Sibson, the man with a problem, had found the solution within himself. The opportunity of war had provided a victorious escape from all dilemmas.

When Wheeler got back to the bridge, White brought him another signal from the *Hecate*. Gray, smoke-begrimed, had been too busy fighting the fire to pay more than short notice to the gun battle. Now he was full of questions.

Wheeler handed him the signal to read. "In view of the late hour, the probability of further damage to this ship, and the necessity to catch the tide off Bloody Foreland, I do not intend to re-embark fire party tonight."

Gray looked at his companion. "I don't blame him," he said. "I'd have done the same. You've got visitors for the night."

157

## Chapter 23

The pall was markedly less. The flames had gone. Then with miraculous suddenness there were only wisps, blue-gray and hazy. For a time the last minutes of the fire's life could be seen in the parti-coloured pillow of smoke that stretched far downwind. Heavy and black where it was furthest from the ship, becoming gray and less dense as it left the tanker. The wind, Murrell thought, never allowed itself to become cluttered with memories. He went into the chart house to write a signal to the Western Approaches Command.

"Attacked by three Heinkels. Two aircraft shot down. No survivors. Remaining aircraft believed damaged. One seaman killed. No material damage to either ship. Am recovering tow." Murrell timed the signal 16.10, and went out onto the deck of the bridge to begin to position his ship for picking up the tow.

They had done this before, and by now the men were used to the work. Even without Gray's assistance the *Antioch* was under way, wallowing comfortably behind the destroyer, by a quarter to five. The doctor, as soon as the hawser was on the towing hook, said, "Shall I take her for a bit while you get squared up? We can argue the toss whose watch it is when you've finished."

"Thanks, Doc," Murrell said, and then, "I'd be obliged if you'd not mention it."

"Eh?" the doctor said, taken by surprise, "Eh?" He paused in the refilling of his pipe. "I'm going to dine out on this yarn for years — whether you like it or not! What the hell do you mean?"

"My — my talking in my sleep." Murrell smiled ruefully. "And I'm sorry I was rude about your bedside manner. Just at that moment — when I was struggling for control of myself — I do believe I'd have preferred a stand-up row. Your sympathy was the last straw."

"Oh, that — forget it!" the doctor said, as between cupped hands he held a match to his warm pipe. The flame singed the wool of his gloves, making a smell like that of a farrier's forge.

Masters passed by them. Murrell called him. "How is the barometer?"

"Down a tenth, sir. *This* anticyclone won't last long."

"The sooner the *Antioch* is in harbour the better," Murrell said. "Come into the chart house."

Together Captain and Navigator bent over the chart. Murrell pushed the deck log to one side. "I want to keep well clear of the land," he told Masters, "even if it does mean a couple of hours more steaming — no cutting corners with our, unpredictable friend astern!" He took a pair of dividers, measured off fifteen miles and pricked the chart that distance north of the Foreland. "I want to pass through that position. Then you can lay off courses to follow the general trend of the coast, keeping fifteen miles offshore until we're right in the mouth of the channel between Scotland and Ireland. Then, if anything happens, we'll have time to deal with it — and sea-room to do it in."

"The Foreland bears green four-five, nineteen miles by radar," Masters said. "I'd like to alter course to oh-eight-three to pass through that position, sir. The wind seems to be drawing a little more northerly." Murrell gave his Navigator a long stare. Now it was all over his officers were taking up their respective duties, and very soon he would revert to being the figurehead again: very soon he would only be able to handle the ship and to make the decisions of a seaman in an emergency or when conditions were difficult.

Desperately tired as he was, he had to admit that in the last five days there were periods, periods that were really quite frequent and long, that had been deeply satisfying. "Very well, Pilot," he said. "Alter course to oh-eight-three." And felt too dispirited to check the Navigator's working-up of the course.

Moving slowly and thoughtfully, he rejoined the doctor. "I began by never daring to hope to see land again. Then I longed for it most passionately. Now I'll be sorry to see it: sorry that this period of intense endeavour is over. Why is that?"

"I'm a physician and surgeon — not a psychiatrist." Macmillan's eyes were blue and amused within their red rims.

"Do I need a psychiatrist?" Murrell asked.

159

"Yes, I think you do — that is, if you are asking for my opinion as your medical adviser. You certainly do if you're going to tell me that you want to go on towing this crate all the way home. Not that I'm the person to go to. I ought to see one too — for I'm damned if I'd hand her over to anyone else now. Come to think of it, the whole ship's company are potential 'cases.' "

"What do you mean?" Murrell asked.

"That we're *all* bloody well balmy!" Macmillan told him. "This thing — this *Antioch* — *has* got under our skins. She's become part of us. She's the symbol of something or other. Oh, when they certify us, they'll find a word for it that none of us will understand — "

"Ships bearing red oh-five." The cry from the port lookout interrupted discussion. Murrell moved to the fore part of the bridge.

"Vessel's signalling, sir," Masters called.

The Yeoman flicked over the pages of the book of pennant numbers. *"Ocean Queen,* sir."

Murrell, through his glasses, could make out the deep scallop-shaped hull; the heavy bridge, far forward; the two flat-sided funnels; the long after deck, so admirably designed for towing; and the white, bustling bow wave that showed under the heavy ropework of the "mouthpiece." If only, he thought, we'd had a fender as big as that, today's damage would never have been done.

A mile on either side of the tug were the lesser dots of the two anti-submarine trawlers. The little party of ships was all of eight miles away. It would be more than half an hour before they met. The tug was signalling. "Slip your tow. I will take over." Already the lamp appeared over-bright against the falling night.

Murrell looked blankly at the signal that the Yeoman held for him. To be ordered about by a blasted tugboat! He saw the look of inquiry in the eyes of the Yeoman. "No, tell him to take station astern," he said, and walked back to the doctor. "If we haven't time to take our own men off that floating deathtrap, we haven't time to transfer the tow."

Macmillan rubbed his pipe against the side of his nose. "Just as you say, just as you say."

Murrell could hear his message being sent, could hear the clickety-clack of the signal lamp. But his mind was too tired to relate the irregular chattering with the words.

The reply to his message came back immediately. "I am ocean tug."

The Captain of the *Hecate* found his mind stiffened with resolve, and found, too, that he had only one thing left to say.

The signalman sent out his three-word answer: SO AM I.

## Afterword

Von Fichte was late returning from his routine visit to the new U-boat pens that were being built in the harbour. He was not late because others had delayed him. He was late because he simply did not want to face the Operations Room and all it had come to mean to him. It was easier to stay among the boats and talk the simple speech to which he was accustomed. One part of himself, the senior officer part, kept telling him to return. The human part suggested a visit to yet one more boat. Von Fichte was surprised at his own humanity.

But not even an admiral could go on doing this indefinitely. The Plot and Spichern had to be faced. It was surprising that he had had no word. He had not wished to make the success of the air strike seem too important by leaving an order that he should be told immediately. He had just hoped that the Chief of Staff would have had the sense to get a message through to him.

It was seven o'clock when von Fichte entered the Operations Room, and the aircraft should have reported back an hour before. But the yellow counter was still on the plot. Each hour, he knew, it had been moved forward, moved nearer to the northwest corner of Ireland that was called Bloody Foreland. It was very nearly there.

The Chief of Staff hurried into the room from his own office as soon as he had heard of the Admiral's return. He stood against the table on the opposite side to von Fichte. The plotting officers came to stiff attention.

"So they have not sunk her?" von Fichte said.

"It appears not, Herr Admiral."

"Have we their reports?"

"They have not returned — yet, Herr Admiral."

"When is their fuel exhausted?"

The Chief of Staff glanced at his watch. "Fifteen minutes ago — but then ..." His voice died away.

"Have we called them by wireless?"

162

"Yes, Herr Admiral, repeatedly — but there has been no reply. The last signal from them was timed 15.55. It read 'Target located. Am attacking.' There has been nothing since."

"And the enemy? Did they break wireless silence?"

"Yes, Herr Admiral. The destroyer made a signal in cipher at ten minutes past four. But not one that was sufficiently long to be reporting damage. There have been no further signals from her."

The Admiral stood for some moments. His hands were clasped behind his back and the fingers laced and interlaced. "Perhaps I should never have given the boat to Lachmann." The speaker hesitated. "But we must not be unfair. We shall never know with what he had to contend." He paused again, lost in thought. The officers waited in complete silence. "Whatever instruments either side may have, they are useless without clearheaded men to work them and a commander to act on the information they give. And thank God that is so, for if ever we reach a stage where valour is not required to fight a war, then mankind will truly have destroyed its own soul. All this means is that this particular Englishman is better than the man we set against him. It is very fortunate for us that the days when great issues could be decided by single combat are past. And yet — heaven knows — small matters may have great repercussions...."

As if his words had pointed his thoughts, his eyes swept around the room. "Where's that fellow Spichern?"

"Herr Spichern has just left, Herr Admiral."

"Left?"

"He is travelling on the seven-thirty train."

"The train for Paris and Berlin! I suppose he knew that the aircraft were overdue."

"I'm afraid so, Herr Admiral. Shall I have him stopped. at the station?" The speaker glanced at his watch. "The train will not yet have gone."

Von Fichte shook his head. "What is the use? The facts on which he will base his building of hate are true. It is only in his representation that there will be errors and distortion. He might as well bear the odium as another."

163

The telephone on the desk behind the Chief of Staff buzzed angrily. He raised the receiver and listened. Then, holding his hand over the. mouthpiece, he brought it down. "Air General Commanding Northwest wishes to speak to Admiral Commanding U-boats personally."

"You take it, *Herr Kapitän,*" the Admiral said. "Tell him I'm out. I'm in no mood to be berated by that ignoramus. Tell him that it was his own insistence on the reconnaissance aircraft that warned the enemy!" He turned and went slowly from the room. The fingers, still interlocked behind his back, worked up on each other.

The Chief of Staff held the phone away from his ears. It bubbled and gurgled. Every now and then he made a wry face and murmured soothingly, *"Jawohl, Herr General."* When, at last, he was able to replace the receiver on its rest, he leaned back wearily against the table. "You can take that damned yellow counter off the plot." He flung the words over his shoulder.

"What did the Air General say, *Herr Kapitän?*" a more senior oberleutnant asked tentatively.

"Putting it briefly, the Herr General said that he was expecting *Reichsmarschall* Goering to lunch tomorrow, and while he's got him there he's going to feed him the Herr Admiral's kidneys on a plate! We can't expect any more interservice cooperation from that source. And — with the trouble the journalist fellow is going to make — there's more than the chance that you may have to get used to the ways of a new admiral. And," he added with personal candour, "of a new Chief of Staff. That damned destroyer has effectively upset the apple cart!"


THE END



**If you enjoyed this book, look for others like it at Thunderchild Publishing: https://ourworlds.net/thunderchild_cms/**

Made in the USA
Monee, IL
14 January 2022